Given by
Judge and Mrs.
Joe Battle
2018

Doe Sia

Amazing Indian Children series:

———————————

The Truth about Sacajawea, is an accurate paraphrase of the Lewis and Clark journal accounts of the remarkable Shoshoni teenager who spent twenty-one months with the Corps of Discovery. The United States Mint used this book when it developed the new Sacajawea Golden Dollar coin.

Doe Sia

*Bannock Girl and the
Handcart Pioneers*

Kenneth
Thomasma

*Agnes Vincen Talbot
Illustrator*

Grandview Publishing Company
Box 2863, Jackson, WY 83001

Fifth printing, November 2009

ISBN: 1-880114-21-6 (Grandview Publishing Company)
ISBN: 1-880144-20-8 (Grandview Publishing Company, pbk.)

Library of Congress Cataloging-in-Publication Data

Thomasma, Kenneth.
    Doe Sia : Bannock girl and the handcart pioneers / Kenneth Thomasma : Agnes Vincen Talbot, illustrator.
      p.   cm. — (Amazing Indian children series)
    Summary: After meeting Emma, who is part of a band of Mormons making their way to Salt Lake City in 1856, Doe Sia, a young Bannock girl, proves her friendship when the two are caught in a brutal snow storm.
    ISBN 0-880114-21-6 (cloth). — ISBN 1-880114-20-8 (pbk.)
    1. Bannock Indians Juvenile fiction. 2. Mormons juvenile fiction. [1. Bannock Indians Fiction. 2. Indians of North America—Wyoming Fiction. 3. Mormons Fiction. 4. Survival Fiction. 5. Frontier and pioneer life Fiction.] I. Talbot, Agnes Vincen, ill. II. Title. III. Series
PZ7.T3696Do   1999
[Fic]—dc21   99-39070

Printed in the United States of America by Cushing-Malloy, Inc.

Grandview Publishing Company 1-800-525-7344

www.kenthomasma.com

**Special thanks
to:**

Larry Van Genderen
orthopedic surgeon and longtime friend
for suggesting that I write this book

Karen Mittan
for allowing me to use the journals
of her ancestor Thomas Moulton,
who with his family traveled with the
Willie Handcart Company in 1856

**The fourth-graders
and fifth-graders in
Dan Thomasma's classroom
Kelly School
Kelly, Wyoming**
for being good listeners
and choosing chapter titles

Melissa Thomasma
my delightful twelve-year-old granddaughter for
her remarkable creative suggestions
and proofreading skills

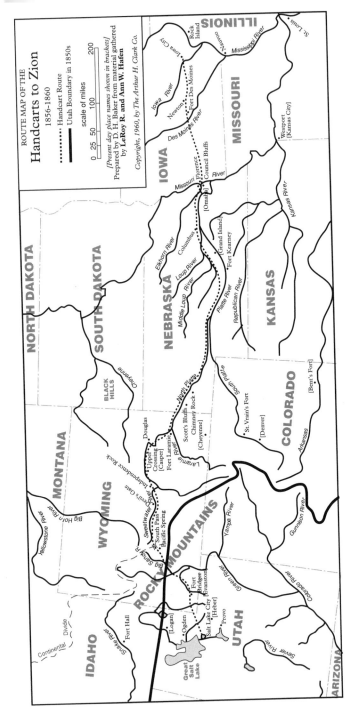

ROUTE MAP OF THE
1856-1860
Handcarts to Zion

········· Handcart Route
——— Utah Boundary in 1850s

scale of miles

0 25 50   100   200

[Present day place names shown in brackets]
Prepared by D. H. Baker from material gathered
by **LeRoy R. and Ann W. Hafen**

Copyright, 1960, by The Arthur H. Clark Co.

Contents

Preface

Many times the native people living in the West encountered pioneers with their covered wagons, handcarts, and herds of cattle. Most of these meetings were peaceful, but a few turned violent. The Mormon handcart pioneers traveling from Iowa City, Iowa, to Salt Lake City, Utah, between 1856 and 1860 recorded their meetings with these native people.

Five handcart companies made the journey in 1856. The fourth handcart company led by Captain

Willie met friendly Bannock Indians in Nebraska Territory. This meeting triggered my desire to write this fictional account of not only the meeting but also the struggles and tragedies the pioneers faced in this historic journey.

The Church of Jesus Christ of Latter Day Saints was founded in 1830. The members of this faith became known as Mormons. The members zealously recruited others to their faith. As a result, Midwesterners began to resent these Mormon believers and a vicious persecution began. It resulted in the death of the beloved leaders of the church.

In 1847 Brigham Young, the new leader of the Mormons, led a group of the faithful across the wilderness to the Great Salt Lake Valley. Here the Saints hoped to live in peace and enjoy freedom of worship.

The church also had a strong missionary presence in England and eventually on the European continent. Many of the Latter Day Saints were very poor. Their hearts yearned for the fellowship of the

Saints in Salt Lake City, their Zion. To help these Mormons realize their dreams, Brigham Young and the church in Salt Lake City established the Perpetual Immigration Fund. The money given to this fund by church members would be used to help the poor Mormons in Europe travel to Zion, and by 1852, the first Saints were given financial assistance for travel to the Salt Lake Valley.

A unique plan was approved by the church in 1855. The poorest of the Saints would be able to go by ship to New York, by train to Iowa City, and then pull two-wheel handcarts while they walked almost thirteen hundred miles to their destination in the Salt Lake Valley. The handcart would carry four hundred to five hundred pounds of food and personal items. Walking fifteen miles a day would get the Saints to Zion in seventy days.

Ten handcart companies would travel this route between 1856 and 1860. Usually there were about five hundred people in a company. Almost three thousand hardy souls made this epic journey. Two of the five companies that attempted the challenge the first year met unavoidable delays and had to travel dangerously late in the season.

Doe Sia is a fictionalized account of the fourth handcart company, commanded by Captain James Willie. All of the events involving this company were carefully researched. The main sources I used were *Handcarts to Zion* by LeRoy R. and Ann W. Hafen (Glendale, Calif.: Arthur H. Clark, 1960) and the journal of Thomas Moulton, who with his wife, Sarah, and seven children made the journey with Captain Willie.

The Bannock Indian girl, Doe Sia, and the Danish people are fictional characters. *Nue Bauee Doe Sia* in the Bannock language means *Snowflower*. To make it easier for children to read, I shortened her name to Doe Sia, pronounced like *doe* (a female deer) *see-ah*.

1

Every Second Counts

It was easy for the young Bannock Indian mother to choose a name for her newborn girl. As the young mother carried her tiny baby from the meadow where she was born, she passed patches of melting snow. There, breaking through the shallow snow, were tiny yellow blossoms of the first flowers of spring.

As the loving mother cuddled her tiny girl in her arms, she whispered, "Little one, I will name you Doe Sia."

In the Bannock language, Doe Sia means *Snow-flower*. As if her name was picked for her in the heavens, Doe Sia would grow up loving snow. As a young girl, she would play for hours in the first snow of winter. Long after other children tired of the games in the snow, Doe Sia would play on alone. It seemed like she was always the last one to get cold.

Doe Sia loved the stories the Bannock elders told when they sat by the fires each night. She heard tales of great courage and amazing survival against overwhelming odds. Her favorite story was about her own family's survival in a snowcave. One winter her mother, father, and grandparents were caught in a sudden massive snowstorm as they traveled home from a short journey. To keep from freezing to death, using their bare hands, they dug into a huge snowdrift and made a room just large enough to protect the four of them from the storm.

This sudden storm raged on for four miserable days. To travel in such a whiteout with windchills far below zero would mean certain death. In the snowcave the body heat of the four adults kept the cave temperature above freezing. Dry buffalo robes provided enough warmth for survival. A small supply of pemmican cakes was enough food for the first two days. When the storm continued on day after day, all the pemmican cakes were eaten. Without food the human body loses its ability to fight the cold and when body temperature slips below normal, death comes in a few short hours. That is called hypothermia.

Doe Sia's grandfather told how the family began to eat pieces of hide. The tough hide was hard to chew and had to be eaten very slowly. If it was not chewed well, the hide would cause severe stomach pain. Every story told by wise elders held lessons for young children to learn. These stories were told again and again. They would never be forgotten.

Ten-year-old Doe Sia stood watching the nearby river rise. Melting snow was causing every stream to flow with great fury. Spring was an exciting season. Doe Sia loved to walk along the river and watch the water roar along its banks. Her dog loved water more than any other dog. Doe Sia named him *Otter-*

dog because he acted like the river otter. He loved to jump belly first into lakes, ponds, and deep eddies in the river. Otterdog was a puppy when Doe Sia was born. The two of them grew up together. Every day they played games that Doe Sia invented just for the two of them. They went everywhere together.

After the trip to the river with Otterdog, Doe Sia returned to her village with a bundle of firewood. As she walked past the first lodge, the girl knew something was terribly wrong. A frantic woman was screaming and crying loudly. Two women were trying to comfort her. Many people were crowded together talking excitedly. Suddenly one by one they left the village and each entered the forest in a different direction. After dropping her firewood, Doe Sia dashed to her mother.

"Doe Sia!" her mother said. "We must help! Little Squirrel is lost! No one can find him! His mother and sister were with him and he just disappeared. They couldn't find him anywhere. He must be found before darkness comes."

Instantly Doe Sia and her mother rushed off to join in the search. They agreed to separate in the forest but to stay close enough to be able to hear each other's shouts. Doe Sia knew all about Little Squirrel. She knew he was always up to something. This three-year-old was curious about everything. His mother knew he had to be watched every minute. This was not the first time he was lost. Fortunately each time before, he was found quickly. Like his name, he moved as fast as a squirrel. One day he found a bird's nest full of eggs. When he brought his treasure to his mother, she made him put it back immediately.

As Doe Sia picked her way through the dense trees following a trail made by deer and elk, she saw no sign of the little boy. She could hear people in the distance shouting his name. She wondered if he would be found in time. With her mind full of thoughts of the horrible things that could happen to Little Squirrel, Doe Sia suddenly stopped in her tracks. There on the ground lay some beautiful shells she had seen just the day before. That was when Little Squirrel was chased by his big sister, grabbed by the arm, and taken to the ground. His sister took her bag of shells from his hand and told him to never touch the shells again.

Doe Sia had watched the whole thing. Little Squirrel's sister walked over and showed Doe Sia the beautiful shells. Now some of these same shells were laying on the ground at her feet. Instantly Doe Sia knew Little Squirrel must have taken the shells again and had gone by this spot. She left the shells where they were and picked up her pace, looking for more shells. She didn't see any more shells but did find one small footprint in the moist soil. It was definitely made by a young child.

Frantically Doe Sia screamed for her mother, but there was no answer. She ran even faster. Dead branches scratched her face and arms. She paid no attention. Nothing would slow her down. Minutes later she broke out of the trees and into an open meadow. Doe Sia slowed to a walk. Carefully her eyes searched the meadow for any sign of the little boy. She noticed a line of broken blades of grass. As she followed this trail, she spotted small footprints where the ground was bare and damp. She was sure she was on Little Squirrel's trail.

Doe Sia knew this meadow. The river was just ahead. The boy's tracks were heading right toward the river. The girl's heart began to beat faster and faster. Now she was in a dead sprint for the river. Could Little Squirrel have fallen into the raging waters? If he did, he would surely drown. The trail ended at the riverbank near one of Doe Sia's favorite spots. She and Otterdog had come to this place often. Most of the year the water here was calm and deep. Every summer Doe Sia and Otterdog would swim and play in the quiet eddy. Now it was a scene of wild white water.

The girl carefully studied the whole area. Her favorite sunning place was a large log that lay across two giant boulders. The log lay propped above the water, three feet from the surface. Doe Sia would leap from the log and splash down next to Otterdog where he swam in the deep eddy. When their swim was finished, both of them enjoyed lying on the log in the warm sunshine. The girl would lie there peacefully stroking Otterdog's head and scratching his ears. Now the log was gone!

Doe Sia dashed to one of the boulders that had held the log in place. She was stunned to find shells laying on top of the huge rock. They were the same shells the boy had taken from his sister the day before.

"Little Squirrel was here! Where is he? What happened to him?" Doe Sia wondered aloud.

Terror filled the young girl. She feared the worst. Doe Sia saw that the second boulder that held the log was under water. Could Little Squirrel have been swept away with the log? Was he already dead?

Suddenly Otterdog took off running downstream at top speed and barking wildly. Doe Sia didn't hesitate. She was in fast pursuit. Did her dog see the boy? Had he found the lost child? The girl's thoughts were running wild. She was jumping logs and rocks and blasting through bushes in a frantic effort to keep up with Otterdog. Something told her every second counted.

Doe Sia leaps into the river in a desperate attempt
to save Little Squirrel.

As Doe Sia rounded a bend in the raging river, she saw Otterdog perched on a fallen tree that hung out over the wild waters. The dog barked loudly. Doe Sia dashed over to the tree to see why her dog had stopped at this place. A terrifying sight met her eyes. There in the angry water bobbed the huge log with Little Squirrel clinging to it for dear life. The log was headed toward a dangerous drop in the river. At the bottom of the four-foot drop, a massive tangle of driftwood and whole trees were held in place by the powerful current slamming them against giant rocks. Little Squirrel's log was on a collision course with the logjam. When he hit this obstacle, the small boy would be swept under and drowned. He wouldn't have a chance.

Doe Sia acted instantly. She jumped to the fallen tree and ran to the far end. Without even stopping, the girl leaped as far as she could into the raging water. With powerful strokes and thrashing legs, the girl battled the icy waves. She angled downstream, using the current to help propel her toward the bobbing log and the tiny boy. The girl was battered and blinded by the choppy waves. She fought on with every ounce of strength in her sixty-pound body. She could not lift her head high enough to see the log. She could only hope that she was on course to reach it in time. Surprisingly she felt her arm slam down on something hard. It was the log! *I made it!* the girl thought. *Is Little Squirrel still here?*

Although her eyes were full of muddy water, Doe Sia clung desperately to the log and tried to see where she was. With all her remaining strength, she kicked and pulled until she was lying stomach down on the back end of the bobbing log. Quickly she rubbed her eyes to clear her vision. She eagerly scanned the entire log. Little Squirrel was nowhere to be seen.

"Little Squirrel, where are you?" screamed Doe Sia. "Oh, no, am I too late?"

Frantically the girl pulled herself on her stomach along the slippery log. Hope was fading. Doe Sia was about to give up when there it was! A small hand was clutching the stump of a branch that stuck out from the huge log.

"Little Squirrel! You're still alive! Hang on! I'm coming!" the girl shrieked.

Without a second to spare, Doe Sia grabbed Little Squirrel's wrist and yanked the small boy from the icy waters. He was trembling violently. His lips were a deep purple. The pitiful child wasn't going to survive much longer. As dangerous tongues of water lashed at the girl, she held tightly to Little Squirrel. She held him like a bundle of firewood under one arm while she clung to the log with her other arm. The log kept dipping and rolling as if it was trying to fling the children off its lifesaving surface. The determined girl with her precious cargo battled with all her strength to stay on the log.

Doe Sia knew their time was short. With every passing second the log was nearing the steep drop. Soon it would slam into the jam of twisted snags and sweep the two of them to their watery deaths. The girl had to think fast. She remembered the words of her father. Every time they entered the river in a dugout canoe, he warned his daughter to be ready for anything. Her father taught her what to do if she was on a collision course with a logjam. She knew she had to be ready on impact to leap from her canoe to the obstacle and let her canoe be swept under without her.

As fast as she could, Doe Sia inched her way forward toward the front of the log. She screamed at Little Squirrel to hang on to her. The little boy sobbed softly. His body quivered with terrible cold and fright, but he clung to Doe Sia with all his might. The girl knew her timing had to be perfect. A split-second of hesitation and a watery death would come swiftly. Now Doe Sia would use the lessons she learned from her father to make a desperate effort to save herself and Little Squirrel. Just as the front of the log came to the edge of the steep drop, Doe Sia lifted Little Squirrel to her chest so he could wrap his arms around her neck.

"Hang on, Little Squirrel, hang on!" screamed Doe Sia.

In an instant the huge log tipped and plummeted down the steep waterslide. The logjam loomed before them. Doe Sia was crouched and ready. The tiny boy clung to her like a baby opossum clings to its mother.

A split-second before the violent collision, Doe Sia rose to her feet and sprang upward. She crashed on the twisted pile of snags. As she held tightly to Little Squirrel, she used her free arm to grab a handhold. Their log had slammed deeply into the pile of driftwood. It whipped around. Much of it was sucked beneath the raging waters. The two children were safe above the river and free of the death trap that the log had suddenly become. The girl's heart pounded violently. Little Squirrel only whimpered as he buried his head in Doe Sia's neck and shoulder.

"It's all right! Everything will be all right," soothed Doe Sia. "We are safe!"

It was true. They were safe for a time, but the girl knew they were still in great danger of losing their lives. There was no safe way to reach shore. The logjam was near the center of the wild river. Little Squirrel's body temperature was already dangerously low. He could not survive the cold much longer.

The boy cried softly, calling for his mother between sobs. Doe Sia had to do something fast. She couldn't just sit there and let this little one die in her arms. At the time it seemed there was no hope of escape. Then Doe Sia heard Otterdog barking. The dog came running to the edge of the river. He began dashing back and forth and barking wildly.

"Otterdog! Go home! Go home! Get help!" Doe Sia screamed.

The dog did not obey. He continued his frantic dashing back and forth. He barked louder than ever. Doe Sia kept shouting, desperately pleading with Otterdog to go for help. The dog did not seem to understand. Why didn't her dog obey? Her hopeless agony made the girl grow more frantic with each passing minute. Doe Sia felt like giving up on Otterdog. She even thought about jumping into the powerful current with Little Squirrel. Maybe, just maybe, she could make it to shore if she took a downstream angle for the shoreline. She knew if she didn't do something soon, Little Squirrel would surely die. Maybe jumping into the angry river was their only chance.

Suddenly everything changed. Otterdog had turned and scampered away from the river. Doe Sia was sure he was finally going for help. She was wrong. Help was already coming! There it was, a wonderful sight! There she was! Doe Sia's mother was running to the river. Behind her came men, women, young boys, and girls! All were shouting at each other!

"There they are! There they are!" everyone cried over and over again.

Little Squirrel's father ran to the riverbank and immediately took charge of the rescue. He shouted to Doe Sia, telling her to hang on. He ordered the men to begin forming a human chain to reach all the way to the logjam. The men grabbed each other's wrists and hung on. With Little Squirrel's father in the lead, one by one the daring men entered the churning water. With their strong legs the men fought to stay standing. The raging water was waist-high and tried to sweep them away.

Man by man the chain was built. Man by man the chain came closer to the waiting children. Little Squirrel's father was the first to reach the logjam. He grabbed hold of a log and shouted to his small son, telling him to climb on his father's shoulders. The little boy obeyed as Doe Sia helped lower him to his father's arms and shoulders. After a few words with his son, the man told him to climb onto the next man. Little Squirrel obeyed as the men drew close enough together so the boy could go from one man's neck to the next. Doe Sia followed close behind to make sure Little Squirrel didn't fall off into the swirling waters.

With both children safely off the logjam, the chain of men began their slow battle to return to the shore. The crowd was cheering them on. The two children came closer and closer to the riverbank. They were clinging to the men for their lives. It was a long, hard struggle for the brave men. Finally the last men covered the final few feet to safety. A great cheer went up as the children were snatched from the men's necks.

Little Squirrel's mother pulled her son into her arms. She was crying for joy! She had a warm fur under her arm. Quickly she pulled the soaking wet clothes from her son and wrapped him in the furry hide. When he was completely dry, she held the boy's small body against her own. This would warm him as fast as possible. Tears of happiness and relief flowed down the mother's face. Doe Sia's mother was there with a warm buffalo robe for her. Mother and daughter hugged each other as everyone was sharing the joy of this great moment.

The story of what happened on this day would be one told by the elders around their fires for many years. A little boy who loves adventure is in danger of losing his young life. A daring and resourceful girl risks her own life to save him. A faithful dog brings help. Strong and fearless men enter a raging river and save the two children from certain death. It would become a favorite story of all children and adults.

Doe Sia was the center of attention for many days. All the children begged her to tell them the exciting story again and again. They liked the part about how she sprang onto the logjam with split-second timing. Doe Sia would never forget this day as long as she lived. She didn't know it, but this very same year she would experience another brush with death and face another attempt to save a helpless child's life.

2

A Strange Smell

Thousands of miles away from Doe Sia's village in the country of Denmark lived another ten-year-old girl. Emma's mother was Danish and had married Emma's father when he came to Denmark as a Mormon missionary from England. Emma had an older brother, Peter, and she adored him. The father taught the family to speak English so the children could speak two languages fluently.

One sad day, about a year ago, Father suddenly died. The family was very poor. They were left with no income. A kind farmer gave them work on his farm and paid them with a place to live and food to eat. Once in a while they were given used clothing the farm family no longer needed. If they worked very hard, Emma's mother would be given a small amount of cash each month. The farm family lived in a large, beautiful home, but money was scarce. Emma's family lived in one room attached to the barn. They had worked to make the room as comfortable as possible.

They missed their father but tried to be happy without him. Together they would play games, tell stories, and sing hymns of the church. Every night Emma, Peter, and their mother held hands and took turns praying. The children always gave thanks for their father and all he had meant to them. They gave thanks for their home, for food, for their good health, and for each other.

Every Sunday Emma and her family walked five miles to the next village. There they met with members of their Mormon faith to sing, pray, and share with each other. Emma loved the walk. She loved being with other girls her age. Sundays were exciting.

It was a cold, rainy Sunday in January 1856 when the family heard the big news. Their walk that day had been chilly and damp. At the church meetings everyone was talking excitedly. Spectacular news had been brought to them by church leaders from England. Emma's mother translated this news to the large gathering. The children were not in the adult meeting to hear what it was. Their mother told them all the details on the way home that afternoon.

"Children, we have a chance to leave Denmark and go to America. Our church elders say we can take a ship to America with many of our fellow Saints. When we get to America, a train will take us to Iowa. Then we will join hundreds of Saints and walk to Salt Lake City. We will pull all of our belongings on a handcart and sleep in tents each night. It will not be easy. Before we decide if we will go, we have to think about it carefully. We must pray about it every day. We will decide together whether or not we will go to America."

Emma listened carefully to these amazing words. Thoughts began spinning through her mind. *Take a ship across the ocean? Ride a train to Iowa? Walk to Salt Lake City?* How could ten-year-old Emma ever understand what all this meant? America seemed like a far-off, wild land. She had never even heard of a place called Iowa.

Peter was the first to speak. "Mother, can we go? Let's go! We can do it! I am strong. I will work hard to get ready. We can have a new life. Father would want us to go if he was still alive. It will be a great adventure. Can we go, Mother? Please?"

"Peter, you are a good son. We will talk about it. We will pray. Our Heavenly Father will lead us."

"Mother, I want to go! I've never been on a ship or a train. Mother, let's go! Please, Mother!" begged Emma.

"My children, we will see. We need time to think about it. Now, let's hurry home before it rains harder."

For the next week Peter and Emma grew more and more excited about going to America. Whenever they had a chance, they talked to Mother about America. They talked about how wonderful it would be to go to America and start a new life. Many of their friends from Denmark would be going. What fun it would be!

The next Sunday morning Mother called them to breakfast. When they sat down, Mother told them she had decided they would go to America. Peter and Emma jumped from their chairs and began dancing around the room. They shouted for joy.

Peter blurted out, "Mother, I will work hard! I will be strong enough to pull 300 kilos. I can go as fast as anyone! America! Here we come!"

Emma hugged her mother and promised that she would be a big help. She said she would help Peter every step of the way. Emma's heart beat with excitement. At church that Sunday everyone was talking about the thrill of going to America. Special prayers were said for all who would be leaving Denmark for America. In the next months more and more information would be shared with the people. They learned the ship would sail from England to

New York. A train would take the Saints from New York to Iowa City, Iowa. The handcart journey would go from Iowa City over twelve hundred miles to Salt Lake City. All expenses would be paid by the church in Salt Lake.

Everyone was instructed to begin getting ready to go. They were told to walk at least ten miles every day to get in shape for the long trek to Salt Lake City. They were encouraged to pray for themselves and for all the Saints who would walk with them.

Peter was serious about training for the trip. He asked the owner of the farm if he could use a farm wagon after all his work was done. When he was told he could, Peter rigged a rope to the wagon tongue. With the rope over his shoulder, Peter pulled the heavy four-wheel wagon from one end of the farm to the other. Soon he could easily pull the heavy wagon up- and downhill.

After Peter was able to pull the wagon smoothly for an hour, he began adding weight to it. He threw sacks of animal feed on the wagon and away he went. Emma saw him add more and more weight every day. One day she begged Peter to let her have a turn to pull the wagon. She could barely move it when it was empty. When it was loaded with grain, she couldn't move it an inch. Emma was proud of her brother. She thought with Peter on the trip nothing could stop them from making it. He could already pull twice as much weight as any handcart could hold.

Everything was going well. Spring had arrived. The earth was turning green. Birds were singing and busy building their nests. Emma was getting more excited every day. Then an unusual coincidence took place. On the same day that Doe Sia saved Little Squirrel from certain death, Emma would also have a brush with death.

It was just before supper when Emma was on her way to feed the chickens. She calmly walked toward the chicken coop daydreaming about her trip to America. Suddenly she stopped. She smelled a strange smell. It was smoke! But where was it coming from? Emma ran to the side of the long barn that stretched away from the farmhouse. There it was!

Smoke was pouring from the workshop at the far end of the barn!

Emma realized she and Old John were the only ones on the farm. Mother and Peter had gone to the village to pick up supplies for the farm. The owners were off visiting friends at the seashore. Old John, the handyman, lived in the workshop. Emma screamed his name, but there was no answer! As Emma dashed for the workshop, she feared the worst. Could Old John be inside? He often napped on his small bed at the back of the shop. Why didn't he answer? Where was he? Didn't he see the smoke?

The smoke was billowing from the partially open single window in the workshop. It oozed from the edges of the door. Emma flew to the door shrieking John's name. Between her calls, she heard a faint cry come from inside the shop. Emma yanked the door open. Instantly she was hit with a blast of toxic smoke. She began to gag and cough. Her eyes watered. She could see nothing.

Emma knows Old John, the handyman,
is trapped inside the burning workshop.

Once again she heard a soft moaning sound. *He's in there!* she thought. *He will die! What can I do?* Emma was tempted to run away from the shop. To go inside could mean certain death! She was always taught to escape a fire and never, for any reason, go back into a burning building. She was taught to go for help. But now the young girl knew Old John's life was in her hands. She was the only one on the farm. She could never find help in time. She loved the old man. He was like a grandfather to her. Now she was his only chance! She had to do something to try to save Old John. She couldn't let him die!

Emma noticed most of the smoke was going up and out the top of the open door. She dropped to her hands and knees and began crawling into the smoke-filled room toward the moaning sound. She shouted John's name over and over, but the moaning had stopped.

Is he already dead? Oh, Heavenly Father, be with Old John. Let him live. Please let him live. Help me save him. I love Old John. Peter, I wish you were here! You wouldn't let Old John die!

Emma squirmed along the floor of the shop. Her stomach was nearly dragging on the floor. She was blinded by the thick smoke. She gasped and coughed and tried to hold her breath. She held one hand over her mouth and nose. Emma crawled forward feeling her way with one hand. It seemed like she would never reach Old John. She desperately tried to remember where everything was in the shop. Breathing was getting more and more difficult. Her throat was burning. She knew she couldn't last much longer.

Just when Emma was about to give up and run for the door, she heard Old John cough. It was the best sound she had ever heard. Old John was right next to her! If he hadn't coughed, she would have passed by him in the thick smoke. Emma quickly reached up and touched John's arm. He felt completely limp.

Between her hacking coughs Emma screamed, "John, it's me, Emma! I've come to help you."

With each word Emma gagged. She realized she could say no more. With all her strength she grasped Old John's wrist with both hands and pulled him off his bed and onto the floor. As he hit the floor, the old man coughed. Emma wasn't strong enough to lift Old John. He weighed seventy kilos. Moving fast, Emma put her arms under his back. With each hand under the man's armpits, she began to drag him toward the door. Breathing was almost impossible as she strained to pull Old John toward safety. She coughed more and more. Her breathing passages burned. Still Emma continued to pull and pull.

It seemed to take forever to drag Old John to the door when it was really less than four minutes. All that time the old man coughed only two times. At least that told Emma he was still alive. That helped her keep going in spite of her misery.

Suddenly Emma felt cool air hit her back. Next she realized she was outside. She laid John down. The girl was on her hands and knees with her head down gulping in fresh air. Never did breathing fresh air feel so good. While filling her lungs with clean air, Emma thought she heard someone calling her name. Maybe she was hearing things. The calling was getting louder and louder. The girl rubbed her eyes and looked toward the farmhouse. When her eyes finally cleared enough, she could see someone running toward her.

"Peter, here I am! Peter, hurry! It's Old John! There's a fire!" Emma shrieked.

Peter sprinted up to Emma, took one look at her, and dropped to his knees next to Old John. "Emma, what happened?" cried Peter.

"Oh, Peter! The shop is on fire. Old John was inside. I dragged him out. Please help him! He can't breathe," Emma gasped between gulps for air.

The frantic girl was still gasping for air when Mother ran to her. "Emma, are you all right? You're covered with dirt and grease! You could have died in there."

The mother held her daughter close to her as Emma sobbed. "I'm all right! I think Old John is dying! Mother, help him! Don't let him die!"

In the next few minutes more people began arriving. Many had seen the clouds of smoke coming from the building. Immediately two men opened the window wide to clear the thick smoke. They found hardly any flames. The fire had started in a barrel of greasy rags. The rags had been smoldering for hours. The toxic smoke had caused all the trouble.

The people fetched a doctor for Old John. The doctor did all he could for the old man, but John was suffering from breathing large amounts of poisonous smoke. The doctor said he would recover, but it would take a long, long time. The men had thrown dirt into the barrel to smother the fire and it quickly burned out. Next they dragged the barrel from the shop. Old John was carried to the main farmhouse for more treatment by the doctor.

When things were under control, Emma was asked to tell what had happened. She couldn't talk fast enough, the words almost tumbled over each other. At the end she told everyone that if she hadn't gone to feed the chickens, she would not have discovered the fire until it was too late. The little girl with the long blonde curls was surrounded by neighbors who stood listening to her tale. Her hair was filthy. Her face was blackened by smoke and grease. Her clothes were badly soiled. Her legs were scraped and covered with dirt.

All the adults told Emma what a brave and daring girl she was. They told her that Old John owed his life to her courage and quick thinking. The next day when the owners of the farm returned, they thanked Emma for saving Old John and their barn. They gave Emma a small cash reward and enough money to buy a new dress, new stockings, and new shoes.

Old John did survive, but his breathing would never be normal again. The smoke had severely damaged his lungs and breathing passages. For many months he was not able to work. Emma visited him every day in his special room in the farmhouse. Old John always told her that she was the bravest girl in the world. Over and over again he thanked her for saving his life.

The day Emma saved Old John's life was the same day that Doe Sia had saved Little Squirrel from a watery death. These two ten-year-old girls who lived such different lives so far apart had no way of knowing that their paths would cross one day in an amazing way and that together they too would have to try to cheat death.

3

March Forth

The winter months had passed so slowly for Emma and Peter. They just couldn't wait to leave for America. It was lots of fun to work on the lists of things they would take with them. They talked about every item. They added up the weight of everything on their lists. Emma asked Peter question after question about the great adventure they were planning. When Peter didn't have an answer, Emma would ask Mother. Emma wondered about the long boat ride across the Atlantic Ocean. She

49

wondered what it would be like to be on the ocean for more than a month. *Where will we sleep? What will we have to eat? What if we have a storm? How will the captain know which way to sail when he can't see land anywhere?*

Emma was full of questions. When she finished her questions about the ocean voyage, she started asking questions about the train ride to Iowa. Next she was asking about the long walk to Salt Lake City. She wanted to know all about the handcart. How would they sleep at night? How long would it take to walk over twelve hundred miles? Would they meet wild animals and Indians? Would there be enough food? Mother and Peter were very patient with Emma. They answered each of her questions as best they could. Then Emma would go over everything in her mind. She began to daydream about the exciting adventure that would start soon.

The great news came on March 12, 1856. Emma and her family would sail on a ship called the *Thornton*. It would sail from Liverpool, England. Each family would need to have their own blankets, bedding, and cooking pots. Food would be provided aboard ship. Mother told her two excited children that the three of them would stay with their Aunt Marie and Uncle Roy who lived in England, not far from Liverpool harbor. This would save them lots of money. They would be close to the harbor and could walk down every day to see all the sailing ships.

On April 10 Emma had to say good-bye to all her friends who were staying in Denmark. She, Peter, and Mother were ready. A ferryboat would take them to England and a train would take them to Liverpool.

Emma was the first one out of bed that morning. The sun was not even up yet. She went to feed the chickens for the last time. As she walked beside the barn in the early morning light, she heard someone calling her name. There in the doorway of the workshop stood Old John. He had his usual smile for Emma.

"Emma, I've been waiting for you. I knew you would come to feed the chickens one more time. Emma, this old-timer will miss you. I will never forget you as long as I live. I will always remember the girl who saved my life. I will miss you, but I know you will have a wonderful life in a new land. I love you, Emma. I wish I could go, too. I have a small gift for you. Here, child, take this with you and remember your old friend as you enjoy each day of your new life."

Old John handed Emma a small cloth bag. The young girl could see a tear in the old man's eye.

"Thank you, John, but you don't have to give me anything."

"My child, I am old. I have no family. Giving you this small gift makes me very happy. I wish I could give you a lot more. I just hope you will remember me in your prayers." Old John's voice quivered as he spoke. Tears trickled down his face.

"I will pray for you every day. I will never forget you," Emma promised.

The young girl gave Old John a long hug as the tears flowed down her cheeks. She tucked the cloth bag into the pocket of her dress and went about feeding the chickens. She never realized how hard it would be to leave the farm.

In all the rush to make it to the ferryboat, Emma forgot about the gift Old John had given her. At the ferry dock she put her hand in her pocket and there it was. She looked inside the cloth bag and found lots of coins. She showed Mother who smiled and helped Emma put the bag in a safe place.

The trip on the ferryboat to England was exciting. There were other families on board who were also headed to Salt Lake City. The train ride to Liverpool was lots of fun for Emma. At Aunt Marie's house Emma's family rested and enjoyed great food. Aunt Marie was an excellent cook.

Every day Peter and Emma headed to the busy harbor to see the huge sailing vessels. Men were bustling about doing their work loading and unloading ships. The day the *Thornton* sailed into the harbor and up to the dock was the greatest day of all.

"Look, there she is! Our ship is here!" Peter shouted. "She's a beauty!"

"Wow! She's huge! Look at all the ropes and sails!" Emma hollered.

A chill flashed up Emma's spine as she gazed up at the beautiful sailing ship. The majestic *Thornton* would be their home for six weeks. Here in the port it looked gigantic. Yet on the vast sea it would be like a tiny speck at the mercy of nature's fury.

After the arrival of their ship, time went fast. Emma and her family used Old John's gift of coins to buy each of them a pair of fine walking shoes and a wool coat and hat. Wool was the best insulation available against the cold. Even when wool is wet, it still retains its ability to keep the wearer warm.

Then there was the health inspection, followed by a check of all the belongings to be taken on board by each family. Emma, Peter, and Mother thanked Aunt Marie and Uncle Roy and hugged them good-bye.

On May 4, 1856, the family walked on board the *Thornton.* To the cheers of the people on shore and over seven hundred passengers, the ship set sail. Out on deck Emma held Mother's hand. Peter stood with his arm around her. They could see Aunt Marie and Uncle Roy waving.

"We're on our way!" Peter cheered. "Salt Lake City, here we come!"

The happy passengers were beginning a journey that would require every ounce of strength and endurance they could muster. Before they reached Salt Lake City, everyone's faith would be put to the test. For some of these brave souls, the cost of this journey would be their very lives. Tragedy would stalk these unsuspecting pioneers and exact a terrible toll from men, women, and children.

Emma found a new friend the first day on the *Thornton.* Katrina was also ten years old and came from a village in southern Denmark. The new friends talked and played by the hour as the ship headed west. For two weeks the ship sailed in fine weather. The sea was calm and blue. When the first icebergs were spotted, the trouble started. A storm blew in from the southwest, churning the ocean into angry waves. The ship began to roll and toss on the giant swells. The people could barely stand and walk.

They had to hold on to something to keep from being slammed down. Like almost everyone else, Emma became seasick. She began throwing up constantly and felt more miserable than she ever had in her young life. Emma laid in her bunk for days, unable to eat or drink anything.

Then, as fast as the storm had come, it ended. The ship stopped rocking and rolling so violently. It took three days before Emma finally felt normal again. At last she could eat and drink and soon she regained her strength.

Everything returned to a normal routine until one day when Emma and Katrina were playing with their dolls. Men and women were shouting. Then the girls smelled smoke. The ship was on fire! Women and children began scurrying to the main deck. Men were already trying to contain the fire. After a long battle, the men succeeded and the fire was extinguished.

James Willie was the president of this company of Saints headed for Salt Lake City. In a meeting after the fire, he told the passengers that much of their food supply had been lost in the fire. He said the elders had to decide on whether they should turn back or keep going. After studying the situation and praying for guidance, the elders decided to continue. A cheer went up from the crowd. President Willie said that now there would be only biscuits and rice for food, but if everyone cooperated, with the Heavenly Father's blessing, they would complete the trip to New York.

It was the middle of June when the *Thornton* sailed into New York harbor. The excited passengers were happy to walk on solid ground again. They were looking forward to good food. Everyone carried their belongings off the ship and put them in wagons that waited to take them and their belongings to the train depot. The fresh food was delicious, but best of all, they could have all the fresh water they could drink. Emma remembered the long weeks of water rationing on board the *Thornton.* Now she and Katrina laughed as they drank and drank all the precious liquid they could hold.

The train ride to Iowa City, Iowa, was especially exciting. The wooden benches were rock hard, but Emma and Katrina paid no attention. They were glued to the windows looking out at all the amazing sights. They had never dreamed there could be so much wild land on the earth. Mile after mile the train rumbled through the vast wilderness. Stops were made at every small settlement. Water was taken on for the boiler-fired steam engine. Everyone on the train talked about the coming journey of pulling handcarts over twelve hundred miles.

As the train rolled on closer and closer to Iowa City, special prayers were said for strength to overcome the challenges that they would face. Emma wondered what the long walk would really be like. She prayed for energy and good health. She didn't want to cause her family to slow down and fall behind. She wanted to do her part and not cause trouble. Emma knew Peter could do anything. He had worked so hard to get ready. Even on the ship Peter had walked on the deck for hours at a time. The captain gave him permission to carry heavy coils of rope on these long walks. Peter was working to build his muscles for the long haul across the wilderness. All the passengers talked about the boy who walked the deck every day.

Bad news was waiting for the people when they left the train and walked to their camp near Iowa City. It was June 26, 1856. The people were told that three days before their arrival, Captain Bunker's handcart company had left Iowa City with every available handcart. Captain Bunker's company was the third group of Saints to leave Iowa City that summer. Now there wasn't even one handcart left for Captain Willie's company.

After the people settled into the camp, a general meeting was called. Captain Willie told them to organize themselves quickly. Men would have to begin constructing handcarts immediately. Women would have to set to work making tents that would be large enough to shelter twenty people. The people would have to work from dawn to dark. Precious time was passing. It was already late in the season. A late start could be dangerous.

In the days ahead Peter worked alongside the men building handcarts as fast as possible. The two-wheel carts would have to carry at least five hundred pounds. They would be loaded with flour, clothing, bedding, cooking equipment, and personal items. The box on the cart would be about four feet long and eight inches deep. The wheels and the axle were the most important parts of each handcart. If not made well, they could be the source of many breakdowns and delays.

Emma and Katrina kept busy helping their mothers and other women sew pieces of canvas together to make large tents, enough tents for five hundred people. The tents would be homes for the people for over four months as they crossed the wilderness.

Katrina whispered, "Emma, these tents are huge. It will be lots of fun to camp out every night."

"They sure are big," agreed Emma. "I hope you and your family can be with us in the same tent. It will be so much fun to be together every night. Maybe we can help each other pull our handcarts."

"The men are making 120 handcarts. Can you imagine what a long line they will make when everyone is pulling theirs?" Katrina asked.

"I'm glad we'll have so many carts and people," Emma said. "Remember, there will be wild animals and maybe even Indians out there somewhere. I wonder if there are any nice Indians. I have heard stories of how Indians have attacked wagon trains and killed people. Just two years ago there was a terrible battle and many pioneers died. I hope we don't ever see any Indians."

"Don't worry," Katrina assured Emma. "Our men are strong and brave. They will protect us. I'm going to stay close to my father. He's strong and not afraid of anyone or anything."

"Katrina, I wish my father was here, but my brother is as strong as any man. He's not afraid. He'll take care of my mother and me," Emma bragged.

"I think Peter is the strongest boy I have ever seen. He is just like my father," Katrina agreed.

At the end of each long day of work, the people met for their evening meal. After eating, they sang hymns and asked the Heavenly Father to bless them and help them with all their labors. Each night Captain Willie reported on the progress of the work. He told how many tents and handcarts had been made that day. He encouraged everyone to keep working as hard as possible.

After two weeks of work, Captain Willie told the people they would be ready to leave in five or six days. The Saints had already been divided into groups of one hundred. The five heavy tents for each one hundred souls would be carried on one of the five wagons being pulled by oxen. Forty-five beef cattle and milk cows would be driven behind the handcarts.

Emma and Katrina were so happy the day they were told they would be in the same group of one hundred and sleep in the same tent with each other. They couldn't wait to get moving. It was July 12 when Captain Willie announced that July 15 would be the day the great journey would begin. Cheers went up from the five hundred Saints of the Willie company. Hymns were sung with great gusto. Fervent prayers

Mother, Emma, and Peter load their handcart.

were offered. People hugged each other and wished their fellow travelers great strength and good health, and a safe trip to Salt Lake City.

"Emma, isn't this great? Finally we are going to start! I'm so happy!" Katrina shouted.

"Katrina, is your little sister feeling better? Can she walk all day? Peter said he can let her ride on our cart if she can't walk all the way."

"Emily is feeling a lot better, but my mother is still worried about her. She is still a little shaky. Emily says she can make it. She's going to rest as much as possible before we start. She is a brave little five-year-old," Katrina bragged.

"Just let us know if she needs a ride. I can help Peter pull her on our cart. Mother says she will push. We can do it," Emma promised.

The night of July 14 was special. The handcarts were loaded. The great journey would begin in the morning. That night everyone gathered for final announcements and speeches. There was joyous singing and powerful prayers asking the Heavenly Father to guide the Saints to Salt Lake City. After all the excitement, Emma, Peter, and Mother walked hand-in-hand to their camp.

It was almost impossible for Emma to go to sleep that night. Thoughts flooded her mind. Could they really pull their loaded handcart over twelve hundred miles? Would there be enough food? Would they have bad weather? Would they meet wild animals? Would Indians attack them? Emma had never walked even twenty-five miles. Now she wondered if she could ever make it all the way. She was sure Peter could do it. He had built up muscles and endurance. He had worked and worked to get ready for this moment. He pulled farm wagons. He lifted eighty-pound sacks of feed. He carried heavy coils of rope all over the ship as it sailed the Atlantic Ocean. Emma knew Peter would never give up. She was sure he could do anything.

When Emma finally fell asleep, she dreamed and dreamed. She dreamed they were pulling their handcart up a steep mountainside. Every time they reached the top there was another peak that was even higher. She dreamed they were surrounded by Indians. Warriors' faces were painted with strange designs. Every warrior carried a spear with a huge shiny point. In another dream Emma was crossing a swift river. Just as she reached the opposite shore, she was met by a gigantic grizzly bear. The angry bear would not let her out of the river. Suddenly Peter walked straight toward the massive bear. Emma screamed for Peter to stop. He paid no attention. When Peter came face-to-face with the bear, he raised his hands to the heavens. He prayed to the Heavenly Father to send the bear away. In an instant the ferocious bear vanished.

Emma woke up shaking. The dream had terrified her. She found herself on top of her blanket and shivering in the cold air. Emma rolled back into her blanket and lay listening to someone snoring loudly. She couldn't get back to sleep for a long time.

In the morning Emma was sleeping soundly. Mother had to wake her. Emma rubbed her eyes as she sat on her blanket. It was still quite dark. People were moving about busily rolling their blankets and carrying them to their handcarts. Peter was already packed. He was helping Katrina's family pack their things away.

Katrina had four brothers and three sisters. They needed two handcarts for all their belongings. Her oldest brother was fourteen, the same age as Peter. Emma and Katrina were happy to be in the same group of one hundred. They would travel together all the way. The two ten-year-olds had no way of knowing that great danger and tragedy awaited all the people in Captain Willie's company. For now they were just two excited and happy friends ready to begin the adventure of their lives.

4

Indians!

Shouts of joy went up as the first handcarts started moving west. Soon the 120 handcarts would be stretched out for three miles along the road to Salt Lake City. Five hundred people would labor together pulling their heavy handcarts loaded with all their earthly possessions. Each handcart carried at least five hundred pounds. The Saints would travel through searing heat, pelting rain, thunderstorms, and many beautiful days.

Right away Peter noticed there were lots of small children and old people in their company. He wondered how the old people would ever make the trip, walking over twelve hundred miles. What if someone died? How could the family keep going? All the people knew there would be great burdens and great hardships to face. Peter had made up his mind to give every ounce of his strength to help those who needed him.

That first morning Emma and Katrina helped Katrina's mother pull one of their handcarts. Little Emily was feeling better and able to walk with her mother. Katrina's father and brothers pulled their heaviest handcart. Peter and Mother were right behind them. The expedition was underway. Oxen hauled the five wagons while young boys drove the forty-five beef cattle and milk cows behind the long line of handcart pioneers. This whole company made quite a sight.

The first day was hot and muggy. The road was good. The people were full of determination, and the day passed quickly. That afternoon Peter and

Mother were the first ones to pull their handcart into camp. Without even resting, Peter headed back to see if anyone needed his help. A mile from the camp Peter found a broken handcart. An old man had it propped up on a log. The right wheel had fallen off. All the baggage was already unloaded. Peter pitched in and helped the man repair the wheel. All the while he noticed the man's wife watching them work. She looked very nervous. She could barely manage a smile when Peter stopped to assist her husband.

Peter had helped build many of the 120 handcarts. He knew exactly how to fix this broken wheel. Soon the wheel was securely in place and ready to roll. Peter helped the old folks reload their belongings. He stepped in next to the man and helped him pull the handcart the last mile to the camp. The elderly couple thanked Peter over and over again. The woman had changed completely. Now she smiled broadly. It seemed as though a great burden had been lifted from her shoulders.

"I'm glad I could help!" Peter said as he turned to leave. "I hope the wheel stays on all the way to Salt Lake City."

"Your son is wonderful," the old woman told Peter's mother. "Our Heavenly Father has blessed you with a good boy."

"Thank you. I am proud of my Peter. He is just like his father. His father would do anything to help anyone in need. Peter truly loves to help others," Peter's mother proclaimed.

That night the Saints gathered for the evening meal followed by announcements, rousing songs, and sincere prayers of thanksgiving for a great first day. They had traveled eleven miles with only a few breakdowns.

Soon every day seemed much like the day before. Up at daybreak, pack the handcarts, roll up the tent, load it on the ox wagon, eat breakfast, grab the handcart, and move out. Camp was always made several hours before dark. The average distance each day was ten miles. It took twenty-eight days to cross Iowa and reach the Missouri River. After a ferryboat ride, camp was made on the west side of the Missouri River near a small settlement called Florence. The company reached Florence on August 11, 1856. By now many handcarts were in very poor condition. Things were so bad that it would take at least a week to make all the needed repairs.

Each and every day while crossing Iowa, the people had seen Peter helping those in need. He helped repair handcarts, he helped pull carts, he even carried a lame boy almost two miles, and did it all with a smile. Everyone talked about this amazing teenager. Off near the river the leaders were having a special meeting to discuss a serious problem. The company was very late getting to Florence. The many delays had used up valuable time. Some felt it would be wise to stay in Florence for the winter. However, most felt they could still make it to Salt Lake City before winter. The leaders were eager to get to Salt Lake City. The elders finally voted five to one to continue their journey. The people were told to be ready to leave on August 18.

Now the handcart company would follow the Platte River across Nebraska Territory. When they came to the fork in the river, the people would go right and follow the North Platte branch of the river. The eager pioneers left Florence and in only a few days they faced many delays. Some of the large wagons broke down. There were serious illnesses and several deaths. The long journey was beginning to take its toll on the weak and the ill. Many tears were shed at the graves of the loved ones who died. Hearts were broken, but the brave souls continued their trek.

One night after the evening meal a tragic event shocked the Saints. It happened close to the Wood River area. Suddenly loud shouts were heard. Men began running. The cattle and oxen were stampeding. A large herd of buffalo had spooked the cattle and oxen. The men did everything they could to stop the wild stampede. It was hopeless! Now darkness covered the land, and the animals were nowhere in sight. The Willie company would suffer a three-day delay while the men searched for the missing cattle and oxen. Thirty animals were lost. Without two oxen to pull each wagon, every handcart had to take on an extra one hundred pounds of flour. This was not a good development for the already late travelers.

Only one day into the trip up the North Platte branch of the river, another surprise awaited the Saints. Terrifying news spread along the line of handcarts. Indians were coming behind them! Many Indian warriors on horseback rode straight for the handcarts. The handcart people quickly pulled their carts close together and waited. Emma and Katrina were shaking with fear. The two terrified girls hid beneath their handcarts.

"Children, stay calm," Emma's mother ordered. "Everything will be all right. Our men will handle things. The Indians may be friendly. If they want food or gifts, we'll give it to them. Stay still and don't panic."

The Indian men had elegant horses. Some wore modern clothes and others wore buckskins. The warriors dismounted and walked toward Captain

Willie and his elders. The two groups greeted each other and even shook hands. These Indian people had met many pioneers who traveled west. They had traded with the travelers, and some even learned a little English. One brave spoke English very well. He had lived with white trappers and was a scout for the United States Army.

As the men talked, Indian women and children came to look at the handcart people. Soon the men found a place to sit in the shade of the cottonwood trees and talk. These were friendly Bannock Indian people who were headed for the Fort Hall area, which was in the same general direction as Salt Lake City. The Indian men were giving Captain Willie and the elders valuable information about the road ahead. The Indian women and children stared at the handcarts and the Saints. They walked all around the handcarts, speaking softly among themselves. They were very curious.

Emma and Katrina were staring at the Indian people and were slowly becoming more relaxed. Emma finally dared to crawl from her hiding place and walk

Doe Sia watches Emma give Otterdog a treat.

out for a closer look. Katrina followed right behind her.

"Wow!" whispered Emma. "These are real Indians, and they're friendly! Isn't this great! I never thought anything like this would happen."

Emma was in for an even greater surprise. As she walked closer to the Indian women and children, she stopped suddenly when a dog ran up to her. She would have jumped back, but the dog was wagging its tail wildly. Then she remembered she had a piece of meat in her hand. The dog sat in front of her begging for a handout. Emma took a look at the piece of meat, shrugged her shoulders, and gave it to the eager dog. He gulped it down in seconds. He continued to sit and beg for more. Emma slowly reached down and rubbed the dog's head and ears.

The Danish girl didn't realize it, but she was being watched intently. A ten-year-old Indian girl stood watching Emma's every move. Emma was petting her dog. The Indian girl was also staring at Emma's long blonde curls. She had never seen a girl with this color hair, since all her people had black hair. Emma continued to pet the dog. When she walked away, the dog followed her.

"Emma, where did you get the dog?" Katrina's little sister asked.

"Oh, he just came up to me begging for a treat," Emma replied.

"Are you going to keep him?" Emily asked.

"No, he's not mine, and we don't have enough food for a dog," Emma explained. The dog followed Emma all the way to a nearby spring. Emma filled a pail with cool water and headed back. The dog trailed behind. Halfway back to the handcarts Emma suddenly stopped. A Bannock girl was standing in the path right in her way. The girl called out, and the dog bolted past Emma. He stopped in front of the Indian girl and began licking her hand. The girl knelt down and stroked the dog's back. She kept looking up at Emma.

"Hello," Emma blurted. "I like your dog. He's friendly."

"My dog is good. He likes you. He does not like everyone. You were good to him. He knows you are good," the Indian girl said slowly.

"Your people are friendly. I was afraid when they said Indian men were coming. You even speak English. Now I'm glad you're here," Emma said sincerely.

"My father speaks your language. We have lived with white people many times. My father works for your soldiers," the girl said. "He is speaking with your men."

Emma and the Indian girl stood by the dog in silence. Neither could think of what to say next. Finally the Indian girl spoke clearly and slowly. "My dog's name is Otterdog. He likes water. He jumps in water and swims as fast as the otter."

"I wish I could have a dog. We are on a long journey. When we get to the end, we will build a home. Then I can have a dog. I love dogs," Emma said. "Otterdog is a nice dog."

Emma noticed that the Indian girl kept staring at her blonde hair. She felt a little uneasy and said nothing for a few minutes. Finally she broke the silence.

"What is your name? My name is Emma."

"My name is Doe Sia. In your language my name means *Snowflower.* I was born when spring flowers were growing through the melting snow. My mother saw the snowflowers and named me Doe Sia. I like snow."

"I like your name. Where I used to live we never had much snow. My country is Denmark. We left there many days ago. Let's walk to the river so I can see Otterdog swim."

Both girls walked to the river with Otterdog racing ahead of them. Before they reached the riverbank the dog had already bellyflopped into a deep eddy. The girls laughed and stood on the bank enjoying Otterdog's antics. Doe Sia called Otterdog back many times so they could watch him jump in over and over again. Emma was having fun but knew she had to get back to her mother. Emma took Doe Sia's hand and motioned for her to come along.

Soon the two girls were back at the handcarts. They could see the men were finished talking, and the Indian people were getting ready to leave. Emma walked to her handcart and pulled out her mother's scissors. In one even motion she took hold of one of her blonde curls and snipped it off. She handed it to Doe Sia.

"Doe Sia, we are friends. I would like you to have this to remember me by. I hope we will meet again someday." Emma had a big smile on her face.

Doe Sia accepted the gift of beautiful hair. She held it in her hand, staring at it intently. Without another word, Doe Sia took a knife from a hide bag that hung from her side. With it she cut some of her long black hair and handed it to Emma.

Emma smiled broadly and said, "It's beautiful! I will keep it in a special place. Thank you, Doe Sia."

"Now we are sisters," Doe Sia declared. "I hope to meet my new sister again."

The girls' fun ended when Doe Sia and her people had to leave. Emma rushed back to find Katrina. Soon Emma was telling Katrina all about her new friend and the fun they had. She showed Katrina the long black hair that Doe Sia had given her.

"Emma, I wish I would have been there. We have a loose wheel. My father and Peter are fixing it. I had to help unload the baggage," Katrina explained.

"I never wanted to meet any Indians; I thought all Indians were bad. Now I have found an Indian friend! This is the best day of the whole trip!" Emma could not contain her happiness.

The Danish girl had no idea what would happen in the near future. Emma would meet Doe Sia again. The next meeting of these two young girls would find them in a fierce struggle to live. These two new friends would have to face death together.

5

Only Time Will Tell

All of the Saints were thankful that the Indian people were friendly. Now once again the handcarts were rolling west. The loss of the cattle was only the first of many things that would go wrong in the days ahead. The North Platte River was very wide. It had many channels and islands. In many places cottonwood trees and bushes lined its banks. The crude road was becoming rougher and rougher with each passing day. The road caused many handcarts to break down. To make the carts lighter, people had to discard many items. Emma's mother decided to leave behind two metal pots, three books, and some of her extra clothes. Peter and Emma also left some of their extra clothes behind.

The rough road was full of ruts and rocks. There were many more hills to climb. One day the travelers looked ahead and saw a spectacular column of rock standing against the clear blue sky. Today this rock is called Chimney Rock. It can be seen for miles. It was a landmark for wagon trains and anyone traveling this historic route.

By this time Katrina's family was having a harder and harder time keeping up. Peter went back every day and helped them pull their two carts into camp. The extra flour that was added to every handcart when the cattle were lost made going slower. Now there was a shortage of flour and even the danger of running out of flour. Still the people were up every morning ready to face another day of hard labor. They all looked forward to their arrival at Fort Laramie where they could get more supplies for the rest of their journey.

As Emma and her mother trudged along pulling their handcart on an easy section of road, Peter ran back to help Katrina's family get up a hill. Suddenly news spread up the line of handcarts. Someone was coming from behind and catching up with Captain Willie's company. Everyone immediately parked their handcarts off the road. Several carriages and two small wagons pulled by fine horses came to a stop and the pioneers gathered around these visitors. They were Mormon church leaders on their way to Salt Lake City.

After an evening meal, there was much singing and celebrating. The church leaders could see that Captain Willie's company needed help as soon as possible. The leaders planned to leave in the morning and hurry on to Salt Lake City at top speed. They would send wagons full of food, clothing, and other supplies to the weary travelers. Fervent prayers were offered, and the next morning at daylight cheers went up when the church leaders sped off for Salt Lake City.

Only a few days later, the handcart pioneers pulled up to Fort Laramie in present-day Wyoming. There was great happiness and relief among the people. They pulled their carts to a camping area near the river. While camp was being made, Captain Willie and the elders went into the fort to inquire about buying flour and other badly needed items. Supplies were low. The people had arrived at Fort Laramie just in time. Everyone was talking about having more food, which would give them much-needed strength to continue on the difficult road. They knew they could do it now.

When Captain Willie came walking from the fort to the camp, the people knew something was terribly wrong. There was no smile on Captain Willie's face. The people learned that the news was very bad indeed. There were practically no provisions available except for some barrels of hard bread. All the supplies had been purchased by the first three companies that had gone this way earlier in the summer. Captain Willie said that everyone would have to eat less food each day. Instead of twelve ounces of flour, now each one would get ten ounces of flour a day. The Captain said it would be necessary to do everything possible to travel more miles each day. He said help would come from Salt Lake City about the time the handcarts reached South Pass. It was critical that they reach South Pass before they ran out of food. The people listened quietly. All were greatly disappointed, but everyone agreed to work even harder. Many talked about trying to make twenty miles each day.

It was September 3 when the Saints left Fort Laramie. Emma's family was up before daylight. They ate a meager breakfast and were the first ones in line to leave. Peter planned to go fast and get ahead. Then he would stop and let his sister and mother rest. While they rested, Peter would head back to help those who were too old or too weak to keep going. He even talked other teenage boys into pitching in to help the weakest travelers.

Now each day was even harder than the day before. The shortage of food made the people weaker and weaker. Every night Peter helped pull the final handcarts into camp. Emma always had his supper ready for him. Her brother was exhausted as he ate his precious food. Peter still joined in the singing and the prayer time.

The nights were getting colder and colder as September became October. In the area of present-day Casper Mountain, the winds were unbearable. Tents were hard to put up in the powerful winds. Some blew down in the night. The Saints couldn't keep warm in their blankets. The people began to wear all the clothes they owned day and night. Sleep was difficult and the misery hard to describe.

The handcarts finally reached the Sweetwater River. Now a miserable crossing faced the Saints. They had to cross the North Platte to reach the Sweetwater. The water was icy cold. Peter and many of his teenage partners made several crossings carrying the old and the sick on their backs to the opposite shore. The crossings were torturous, but somehow everyone successfully reached the other side. Now they could follow the Sweetwater River to South Pass.

Each morning was worse than the one before. People were weary from lack of sleep and lack of food. They shivered in the bitter cold. Emma couldn't wait to get moving. Her feet were cold. She would look at her shoes, her wool coat, her wool hat, and remember Old John and his gift. She wished she could tell him how much the shoes and coat and hat were helping her now. Emma wished she could give Old John another hug and tell him she loved him and thank him again for his wonderful gift.

Captain Willie's handcart company had slowed to less than ten miles a day. They would never make it to South Pass before they ran out of food. Yet the people plodded on and prayed that help would come in time. Emma felt weak, but she always did her best to help pull their cart. Her whole body ached. Her stomach always felt empty. She started daydreaming about food and a warm bed. Emma wondered how much longer she could keep going. Every night Emma and Mother lay huddled next to each other, sharing their blankets. They kept their coats and all their clothes on, but even this could not keep out the bitter cold.

The days were utter agony. Still the people struggled on and on, one step at a time. Every day someone died and had to be buried. Some days several people died. The sadness touched everyone. One man pulled his handcart all day only to die in his sleep that same night. Emma could not bear to see children crying their hearts out at the death of their daddy. Emma knew how sad it was to lose her own father. Every night Emma hugged Mother and kept asking if she was all right.

"My little Emma, I will never leave you. All of us will make it to Salt Lake City. Every day we will be close to each other. The Heavenly Father is with us," Mother assured Emma. "We will make it. All of us will."

The unbelievable agony continued. All up and down the line of handcarts the people were weary, hungry, and cold. The young men were becoming exhausted. More and more people were falling behind the main group. Even Peter had slowed down. He was not getting enough food to maintain his strength. The suffering travelers had passed Independence Rock and Devil's Gate. Finally the most horrible day of all came. On October 19 the last ounces of flour were passed out to the starving people. Now death by starvation was a real threat to these miserable souls.

The travelers stopped at noon on October 19. Snow had begun to fall. Icy cold winds swirled the snow into the faces of the people. Everyone huddled behind their handcarts for protection from the icy blasts. Captain Willie had saved the barrels of hard bread for just this moment. He ordered the bread to be passed out to his starving company of Saints.

While the travelers rested at noon, a wonderful surprise greeted them. Joseph Young and Cyrus Wheelock drove their light wagon up to the handcarts. They had come from Salt Lake City and had great news. Sixteen loads of supplies were on the way. Joseph and Cyrus begged the Saints to keep going. With Captain Martin's company even farther behind, there were over one thousand people who needed to be rescued. Even sixteen loads would not last long for that many people.

Emma had not seen Katrina and her family all morning. She was worried about Katrina. Katrina was hurting so badly the day before that she had to be helped to camp.

Emma pleaded, "Mother, I want to go find Katrina. I want to give her some of my bread. She is so hungry. She could hardly walk yesterday. Please let me go back and give her some bread. I can help her catch up."

"Emma, it's cold. Katrina will be all right. Her mother will give her bread. You need to rest. We have to pull our cart all afternoon."

"Oh, Mother, I haven't see Katrina all morning! She must be way behind! Maybe she won't get here in time to get some bread. I know she's hungry now. Please let me go back and give her some bread. Please, I have to go find her. I know she needs me! I'll come right back. Please let me go!" Emma begged.

"Well, all right, Emma, but be sure to be careful. If you can't find her, come right back. We have to leave here soon."

"Thank you, Mother. I'll be back on time. Don't worry."

Emma stuffed her hard bread into her coat pockets, stood up, and left to find Katrina. She had no idea that she would not be able to keep her promise to her mother. She had no idea that soon she would be facing a lonely death. No, she would not be right back.

Emma walked away from the noon rest stop and headed back down the road. She eagerly checked every handcart she passed. She asked all the struggling people if they had seen Katrina's family. No one had seen them. Emma was sure that any minute she would find Peter helping Katrina's family catch up. Peter never had to ask his mother if he could leave to help others. He did it every day.

As Emma walked along the road, the wind began blowing even harder. Snow swirled over the landscape. Emma could barely see the tracks the hand-

Emma struggles alone in a blizzard.

carts had made. The road was rapidly filling with snow. She couldn't even see the nearby mountains. It was a complete whiteout. The girl should have turned back immediately. Just when Emma was going to give up finding Katrina and turn back, she came to a handcart pulled by two young men. They told her Peter was less than half a mile farther on. Emma was so relieved. Now she pressed on through the blinding storm even faster.

"Only a little way farther. I can make it. I can do it. Katrina needs me. I know it," Emma mumbled.

After only a short distance, the girl's pace slowed. Now she was wading through deep snow-drifts. Soon the fresh tracks just made by the hand-cart that passed her were filled with snow. Emma couldn't see a thing. Her hair was caked with snow. Her eyes were watery. Still the determined girl kept going. She was so sure she must be near Peter by now. She began shouting his name over and over again. The roaring wind muffled her calls for Peter. When there was no answer, once more Emma decided to turn back. Now it would prove to be too late. She had already wandered off the road. When she turned to go back, she actually was heading farther away from the handcart road. She had lost all sense of direction.

Emma had no experience at wilderness survival. She did not know the rules of survival in such a horrendous blizzard. The first rule is that the lost person should stop immediately. This way he or she does not become more lost than ever. By stopping immediately Emma might have a chance of being found. Instead, with each step she took she was becoming more and more hopelessly lost in this horrible whiteout.

Screaming Peter's name louder and louder, Emma panicked. The howling wind was her only answer. The bitter cold penetrated her wool coat. She began to shiver violently. She began to stumble and fall. It was becoming harder and harder to get to her feet. She was losing all sense of time.

"Oh, what am I going to do? Mother! Mother! I need you," Emma sobbed. "Where am I? Oh, Heavenly Father, I want my mother! I'm so cold and hungry! Please help me!"

Emma could barely move. Still she stumbled on blindly. Without warning she came to an abrupt stop against a wall of rock. She was far, far from the handcart road. The rocky slope rose in front of her into the snowy clouds.

"Where am I? Oh, Mother, I'm not going to make it. I can't see. I can't find my way. I'm freezing. I can't go on. Oh, Heavenly Father, don't let me die. Please help me find my mother. Please," Emma prayed.

In her misery Emma slumped against a giant boulder. She shook uncontrollably. She felt weak and completely helpless. With the energy she had left, she decided to make a final try at walking. Somehow she had to outlast the storm. She began to pray for the storm to stop. Emma's feet were so cold that they ached with horrible pain. She began to stomp her feet. Then she began moving again. She followed the hillside walking step-by-step like someone in a trance.

Without knowing it, Emma was headed to a life-saving shelter. She stumbled forward into a massive boulder. She walked around it and found it was a place where three boulders had tumbled down the mountainside and landed right next to each other. The boulders were leaning against each other, creating a triangular shelter between them. Emma crawled into this haven for protection from the wind and snow. For the first time that day she was protected from the biting wind. The relief was instant. Emma's eyes began to clear. She could actually see again. She wasn't warm but at least was able to brush the snow from her clothes, dig the snow from her hair, and rest against the boulder. The discovery of this shelter had come just in time. Emma would not have survived much longer in the roaring blizzard.

"Thank you, Heavenly Father. Thank you for leading me to this shelter," Emma cried out. "Please let the storm stop. Please help me. I want to go back to my mother."

Without shelter many lost people have died in a matter of a few hours. Emma's body temperature had already started dropping. Soon her blood would thicken and then stop moving. Hypothermia would eventually lead to death. At least now Emma had a better chance of survival for at least a few more hours. Her only chance was for the storm to stop and for searchers to find her in time. But would the storm end in time for Emma to be rescued? Would she ever see Peter and Mother again? Only time would tell.

6

Desperate Decision

The rocky shelter was large enough for Emma to stand up in, and it protected the freezing child from the wind and snow but not from the bitter cold. She began to stomp her feet to improve her circulation. She shivered uncontrollably. She kept her hands and arms under her wool coat with her hands in her armpits. Then she realized how hungry she was. Emma put her hand into her coat pocket and felt the hard bread still there. Now this meager supply of bread would become the difference between life and death for her.

Emma had stumbled into a lifesaving shelter. She also had lifesaving bread to allow her body to generate some inner body warmth. Without these two things her body temperature would drop even faster. At first Emma thought about saving her bread for Katrina. After thinking it through, she realized she might never find Katrina in time. Katrina was probably back at the handcarts already. In her freezing cold shelter, Emma chewed on the chunk of hard bread. It tasted so good. It even took her mind off her misery for a few minutes. Her thoughts turned to Mother and Peter. Were they all right? Did they know she was lost? Would they come looking for her? Had the rescue wagons come with food, blankets, and warm clothes?

"Mother, I pray that you and Peter are all right. I hope you don't worry about me. I'm alive. Somehow I will find my way back to you, I promise!"

Emma's words made her feel better. The bread was helping her body regain a little warmth and strength. She truly believed she would make it back alive. She promised herself that she would never give up. Emma watched the sky grow darker. The storm raged on with over a foot of snow already on the ground. Emma was now faced with a long, long night of numbing cold and misery. She decided to save half of her bread for the next day. She was sure she could make it back to the handcarts as soon as the storm ended.

She began walking in small circles in her cramped shelter. Emma wisely knew she would have to keep moving to stay warm. When she became exhausted, she laid down in a dry place next to one of the boulders. She didn't dare sleep because she was afraid she would never wake up. Each time she laid down, she curled up so her coat covered even her feet. To stay awake she sang songs of the church and talked to Mother and Peter like they were there with her.

The time dragged on and on. It seemed like the miserable night would never end. Several times Emma dozed off into a fitful sleep. Each time she did, she woke up shaking terribly.

"No! I can't sleep. I'll die! Dear Heavenly Father, please help me to stay awake. Please let the daylight come soon. Please let the storm stop. I want my mother. I love her. Please help me, please."

Every few minutes Emma peered between the rocks to see if it was daylight yet. The sky seemed like it would remain pitch black forever. The storm became worse than ever. The wind howled as the heavy snow fell at over an inch an hour. It seemed like the horrible night would never end.

Finally Emma could see the darkness begin to give way to daylight. Emma was very weak and bitterly cold. She ached all over. She took the last of the bread from her coat pocket. She decided to eat only half of the tiny amount that was left and save the rest for her trip back to the handcarts. There was no change in the storm. Blowing snow made it impossible to see more than ten feet. This left Emma with a critical decision. Should she stay or go? It would be a desperate choice, one that could mean life or death.

Emma made the wrong choice. She decided to leave even though she could not see even ten feet in the blinding blizzard. In her desperation she decided to leave her lifesaving shelter and try to find help. She decided to walk straight away from the rocky hillside. She thought that walking this way would take her back to the handcart road or river. If she found the river first, she planned to follow it to the handcarts. Somehow she thought she could make it.

After she said a prayer, Emma ate half of her bread. She stuffed the leftovers in her coat pocket and wrapped her wool coat collar tightly around her neck. She pulled her hands up into her long coat sleeves and walked out into the storm. The blast of cold wind seemed to go right through her small body. She had several layers of clothes on but she still suffered from the severe cold. It felt good to be moving. Emma had great hopes of finding Peter and Mother before this day ended.

With nothing to guide her on a straight course, Emma was soon going the wrong way again. Without realizing it she was getting more and more lost and even farther away from her family. Walking became harder and harder. She was plunging through knee-deep snow. Somehow the desperate youngster kept moving.

"Mother, I'm coming. Please be close by. Mother, I need you. I'm alive. Oh, Heavenly Father, help me find my mother. Make the storm stop. Help me keep going. Help me make it. Oh, I have to make it," Emma stammered.

Emma had no way of knowing that her body temperature was gradually going down. She was becoming a victim of a killer, hypothermia. When body temperature drops below ninety degrees, blood circulation changes. When the brain doesn't receive enough oxygen, the person loses the ability to think clearly. A false feeling of warmth comes over the one who is actually freezing to death. When this happens, death is only a matter of a few hours away.

Somehow Emma managed to plod on through the deep snow. She paused to eat the last pieces of her bread. It would help fight off certain death for a short time, but Emma's time was running out. She was hopelessly lost. Her mother and all the others were nowhere near this doomed child. Already much of this day had passed with no chance of success for the desperate girl.

As Emma struggled to keep going, she began to slip and fall. Each time she fell, it became harder and harder to regain her footing, stand up, and keep going. Emma was fast losing her strength and the ability to keep her balance. Now she was falling every few minutes. She could barely walk. Now getting up was becoming nearly impossible. Without finding shelter soon, Emma would surely die.

Emma was also losing her ability to think clearly. She started hearing sounds when there were no sounds. She even thought she could see handcarts just ahead of her. She was sure she heard Peter calling her name. She even shouted back to him. Her mind was playing tricks on her. Her circulation had slowed down so much that she could no longer think rationally.

As the delirious girl took her final steps before collapsing for good, amazingly she stopped next to a huge fallen tree. She touched it. She was sure it was the wood on a handcart. She thought she had made it back. She thought she was safe. The helpless girl slumped to her knees and rolled over to lie next to the tree. She was sure she was rolling into her bed back at the farm in Denmark. Now without a miracle Emma would go to sleep in this place and never wake up. No one would ever know how her life ended in this horrendous storm. No one would ever know the tremendous fight this girl had fought to find her mother and Peter. So far from Denmark, Emma's death would be a lonely and tragic end for a loving daughter and sister.

Emma felt warm and cozy even though her small body would soon give up its fight against hypothermia. In less than ten minutes, Emma fell into a deep sleep. Death would soon visit this young girl. When all seemed completely hopeless, the unpredictable happened. A brief break in the storm occurred. The day brightened for a few precious minutes. That was

Doe Sia and Otterdog spot Emma lying in the snow.

all that was needed for a miracle to happen. This would prove to be a lifesaving moment for Emma. High above the dying girl another girl stood wrapped in her buffalo robe. A dog stood by her side. Miraculously this girl was Doe Sia with Otterdog.

During the snowstorm, the Bannock Indian girl had also been caught in the whiteout. With Otterdog curled up with her in her buffalo robe, the two of them had survived the violent weather all night long. When the storm cleared for these few minutes, Doe Sia came to the edge of the ridge to look for landmarks that would lead her back to her people. She was shocked at the sight below her. There, next to a fallen tree, lay the girl with the long blonde hair. Immediately Doe Sia could tell that Emma was either dead or dying. She knew she had to do something. She knew the Great Spirit had put her here in this place and at this time to help her friend. Doe Sia's people taught her that everything happens to a person for a reason.

Without wasting a second, the Indian girl found a way down the steep slope. She reached the bottom of the hill just two hundred feet from Emma. The break in the storm had already ended. Again heavy snow was falling even faster than before. Doe Sia plowed through the deep drifts. When she hit the fallen tree, she made her way to the dying girl. Doe Sia brushed the snow from Emma's hair and face. Emma lay in a deep sleep. She was dreaming that her mother was waking her up. Doe Sia screamed Emma's name over and over.

Emma mumbled, "Mother, I'll get up. Just let me lie here a little longer."

Doe Sia realized that something was terribly wrong. Emma was not thinking straight. She grabbed the girl by the arms and pulled her to a sitting position.

"Emma! Emma! Wake up! It's me, Doe Sia! It's cold! There's a storm. We will die here!" shouted Doe Sia. "You must stand up! I am here to help you."

Emma could only stare straight ahead. She was numb and cold. She had no idea what was happening. She had no idea that someone had come to help. Doe Sia acted quickly. She pulled off her buf-

falo robe and laid it on the snow. She lifted Emma
to her feet. She held one of Emma's arms around
her own neck to keep her from falling. With her free
hand she brushed the thick snow off Emma's coat.
Doe Sia worked hard and fast.

When Doe Sia had Emma as free of snow as possible, she pulled off her wool coat and rolled the
delirious girl into the fur of the buffalo robe. The
Indian girl immediately began digging into the side
of a massive snowdrift. She dug as fast as possible
with her bare hands. Soon she was all the way in
the snowdrift where she began carving out a small
room. She was careful to make the snowcave just
large enough for two girls and a dog. Doe Sia worked
frantically. Otterdog was so excited that he was digging away at the snow right next to his master.

"Good dog! Good dog!" gasped Doe Sia.

As soon as the girl had made the room large
enough, she trudged through the snow to Emma.
Doe Sia grabbed the end of the hide and dragged it
and Emma right to the opening of the snowcave.
The Indian girl crawled backward into the cave and

pulled Emma in with her. Doe Sia had put the wool coat on the floor of the snowcave for insulation. Otterdog clamped his jaws on the hide and tried to help pull.

"Good dog! You're helping!" shouted Doe Sia.

Once inside the snowcave, Doe Sia caught her breath. She had been working at top speed for thirty minutes without rest. She brushed all the snow from her own body and dress. Then she unrolled the huge buffalo robe, and she laid down next to Emma. Doe Sia pulled the sides of the robe over them. The hide was just big enough to cover them. Doe Sia made sure Emma was completely covered. The wool coat helped keep the cold of the snow from penetrating the buffalo robe.

The snowcave served to block all the wind and blowing snow. Doe Sia had made the opening just large enough to crawl in and out. The three bodies would gradually give each other lifesaving warmth. The temperature in the snowcave began to rise and would go a little above freezing.

Doe Sia heard Emma moan softly. This told her the Danish girl was still alive. In the cramped space, moving was difficult. Doe Sia managed to change positions regularly. She wanted to hold her body close to Emma on all sides of the freezing girl's body. This would help warm Emma on all sides. Doe Sia remembered surviving a snowstorm with her family when she was only six years old. They, too, dug a snowcave and huddled together to keep each other warm. Doe Sia never forgot how warm her mother's body felt as they lay as closely together as possible. Now she knew she had to do the same thing for Emma. She had to try to save Emma's life.

The relentless storm continued with even greater fury. Anyone looking down at this scene would say it looked absolutely hopeless. The snowcave was tiny. It was surrounded by gigantic snowdrifts. Inside lay two young girls and a dog. One girl remained weak from her brush with death and could still die. These two girls from completely different families and different ways of life were now in a struggle to survive against great odds. The storm that had seemed so powerful would never stop. Now another miracle would be needed to save these two young friends. Would that miracle come in time, or would this snowcave become the girls' final resting place? The hours ahead would hold the answer.

7

The Beginning of the End

When Emma didn't return to the handcarts, Peter and Mother frantically searched for her all day. They found no trace of her anywhere. Her mother and brother had all they could do to stay alive in the freezing storm. Everyone told them they would have to give up and keep going, or they themselves would die. At the end of the day Peter and Mother stood next to their handcart and hugged each other and prayed for a miracle for their little Emma. They hoped that Emma had been found by someone in the Martin company, which was coming up behind Captain Willie's company. Emma's mother was blaming herself for allowing her daughter to leave to look for Katrina.

The agonized mother prayed, "Heavenly Father, my dear little Emma only wanted to give some of her bread to her friend. Why is this happening to my little girl? I love her. Heavenly Father, please take care of Emma wherever she is. Bring her back to us, please. I love her so much. She deserves to live. Please protect my little girl."

Meanwhile, Doe Sia, Emma, and Otterdog lay huddled together for hours. The day had ended and the storm roared on into the night. Emma's body temperature had begun to rise ever so slowly. Her soft moaning had stopped. Doe Sia could hear Emma's breathing become steadier and deeper. The temperature in the snowcave was cold but still much warmer than the outside air. All through the night Emma's condition slowly improved.

Doe Sia could tell Emma was doing better because Emma moved when Doe Sia moved. They huddled close together for a while and then moved to a new position. This way they kept even warmer. Otterdog lay at their feet under the buffalo robe adding his body heat to keep the girls warm. A little before daylight Emma muttered her first words.

"Where am I? Mother, are you here?"

"Emma, you are all right. I am Doe Sia. We are lost. I found you. We will live. We must stay here and keep warm," Doe Sia whispered.

Emma did not answer. She did not understand the Indian girl's words. Nothing made sense. Had she died? What had happened? Emma lay there trying to understand the words she had just heard.

Finally, Emma spoke. "Who are you? Why are you here? Where is my mother?"

"I am Doe Sia. I found you dying in the storm. I dug this snowcave. We are in my buffalo robe to keep warm. Your mother is not here. We will find her. I will help you. We must wait for the storm to end."

"Storm? Is there a storm? How did I get here? Where is Peter? Where is Mother?" Emma was frantic.

"Emma, we are alive! We will live! We will find your people. You must listen to me. The snowstorm can kill. We must rest now. We must keep warm. We will talk later."

Doe Sia knew Emma was not thinking clearly. She knew the girl might do the wrong thing. She might start out in the storm and end up frozen to death. Doe Sia decided to keep Emma from doing anything that would endanger her life. She knew it was up to her to take charge of every move they would make.

The girls became quiet once again. They huddled together sharing their body heat. As daylight came, Doe Sia could see the storm was as strong as ever. The wind was howling. Snowfall continued as heavy as ever. Some snowdrifts were six- and eight-feet deep. The Indian girl knew that certain death waited just outside the snowcave. There would be no leaving until the storm cleared.

Doe Sia pulled a hide bag from underneath the buffalo robe where she had stored it. Inside the bag were four precious pemmican cakes. These cakes, made of meat, berries, and seeds, were the only food the two girls had. Emma's bread was gone.

"Emma, can you hear me?" Doe Sia asked.

"Yes, who are you?" Emma replied.

"I am Doe Sia. I am your friend. Many days ago I saw you on the road. You saw Otterdog. You gave me some hair, and I gave you hair. We are friends."

"Doe Sia? Otterdog? I want my mother," cried Emma.

"Emma, we must eat. We must be strong. We can live if we help each other. Here, eat this food," Doe Sia ordered.

Doe Sia handed Emma a pemmican cake. The girl slowly moved her hand to take the cake. When she tried to hold it, it fell from her fingers. Emma could barely pick it up. Her fingers were still numb from the beginnings of frostbite. Finally, with Doe Sia's help, Emma held the pemmican in her hand. She stared at the strange-looking cake.

Doe Sia spoke. "You must eat! Eating will give us strength."

Doe Sia hands Emma a pemmican cake.

Emma looked at Doe Sia and smiled. This was the first sign that Emma was recovering from her devastating ordeal. She was still very confused, but she was slowly returning from the brink of death. Emma ate the whole pemmican cake. She brushed her hair back from her face and laid down again.

"Oh, I'm so tired. How did I get here? Where are we? How did you find me? When can I see my mother and Peter?"

Doe Sia told Emma the whole story again. She went on to tell Emma about her plan to help her find her people.

"We must stay here until the storm ends. When it is safe to leave, we will find your family. Now we must eat and drink. The snow will give us water. We will eat pemmican, and then we can eat pieces of hide. We will not die."

Emma lay listening to Doe Sia's words. Before she could even think about her questions, the weak girl dropped into a deep sleep. Doe Sia carefully covered Emma right up to her ears. Otterdog crawled out of the snowcave and returned after a few minutes. He squirmed into his place in the buffalo robe.

The storm continued as powerful as ever. The snowcave blocked all the wind and snow. The tiny room remained above freezing. As long as the girls stayed in their shelter, they were warm and safe. It was so warm in the snowcave that water dripped from the ceiling. Soon all was still once again. The girls slept well for five hours.

Doe Sia woke up early that afternoon. She crawled from under the buffalo robe and stuck her head outside. Snow was still falling, but the wind had died down. The Indian girl smiled. This could be the beginning of the end of the storm. Doe Sia crawled back into the snowcave and back under the buffalo robe. An hour later Emma woke up. Her eyes were no longer blurred. Now her eyes were clear and bright.

"Where am I! How did I get here? Where is my mother?" Emma cried frantically.

Doe Sia realized that Emma had remembered nothing she had told her. At last Emma seemed to be acting normally. She seemed ready to listen, understand, and remember. Patiently Doe Sia told Emma the entire story again. This time Emma looked at the Indian girl the whole time she was talking. This time Doe Sia was sure Emma could understand everything she was saying. When Doe Sia told Emma that she would help her find her mother, Emma's face brightened.

"Can we find my mother and Peter? When can we start? Can we go now? I want to go now. My mother and Peter will be leaving, then I will never find them. Let's go now. Please, can we find my mother today?"

"Emma, the snow still falls. The wind is gone. Tomorrow we will go. We will travel like the animals do. We will find the easiest way. We will walk where the snow is shallow. Now we must eat and rest. We must be ready to leave when Grandfather Sun returns."

Doe Sia gave Emma another pemmican cake. She also cut strips of hide for food.

"Eat this pemmican. It will keep us alive. It will give us strength. Then we will eat hide," Doe Sia said.

Emma didn't hesitate. She eagerly ate the second pemmican cake. She took some hide and began chewing it. She was so hungry she would eat anything. The girls lay in the warmth of the hide enjoying their pemmican and chewing the tough and tasteless strips of hide.

Far from the snowcave the Willie handcart company was suffering and in utter misery. They had not moved a step during the storm. The leaders knew that if they moved even more people would die. They decided to stay in camp and wait for help to arrive. The day Emma became lost, she had survived the first night alone protected by large boulders. At the end of the second day Doe Sia found Emma next to the fallen tree and near death.

Day three of Emma's disappearance would be a great day for the Willie company. At sundown a glorious sight appeared on the crest of the hill above the handcarts. Two large wagons, pulled by two teams of majestic horses, were coming toward the group. The wagons would be full of food, warm clothes, wool socks, and stacks of blankets. Joyous cheers shot up from the handcart people.

Immediately fires were built and food was cooked. Clothes and blankets were handed out. The camp abounded with great joy and celebration. The people had been saved! Emma's mother hung her head and began to cry. Peter gently hugged his mother. He didn't know what to say.

His mother sobbed, "Why didn't this help come sooner? Why didn't help come in time for my little girl? Oh, darling Emma, where are you? Are you still alive?"

Elder Kimball heard Peter's mother crying and came over to her. Peter had already told him about his sister. He had explained every detail to Elder Kimball. The kind man told Peter and his mother that he understood their tears. He promised that as he moved back down the road, he would check every handcart along the way. He explained that there were still handcarts stretched out for miles behind Captain Willie's company. He said Emma could have been found and be safe with another family.

"If we find Emma, we will bring her to you as fast as humanly possible. Peter, you must help your mother. Both of you need to pray for Emma. Prayer is powerful. Miracles still happen. I must go now. May the Heavenly Father bless you both." With those kind and hopeful words Elder Kimball turned and left.

"Mother, I have been praying for Emma day and night. Emma is a good girl. The Heavenly Father will take care of her. I love my little . . ." Peter could not finish. He broke down in tears. His mother hugged him tightly.

"Peter, it will be all right. You are a loving brother. We must pray together. Emma is either alive or she is in heaven. We need to put Emma in the Heavenly Father's hands. He knows what is best for her."

"I'm all right, Mother. I'm all right," Peter sniffed.

As the sun went down behind the western horizon, the girls' snowcave was in the shade. Once more Doe Sia crawled through the opening to the outside. She stood up and a broad smile broke across her face. She quickly dropped to her hands and knees and squirmed back into the snowcave.

"Emma, the snow has stopped! The storm is over! We can leave in the morning!" Doe Sia shouted.

Emma quickly crawled from the buffalo robe and squirmed through the opening. She slowly raised herself to a standing position. Her legs wobbled under her. She felt dizzy. Her head ached. She stood unsteadily in one place. She could see the storm had ended. Everywhere she looked she saw huge snowdrifts. Emma didn't recognize any landmarks. She had no idea which way they should go to find the handcarts. She wondered how they would ever find her mother and Peter. She wondered if her family was still alive. If they were alive, had they given up on finding her? Had they left for Salt Lake City thinking she was dead? These thoughts raced through her mind.

The longer Emma stood up, the less her legs shook underneath her. Yet the girl felt very weak and woozy from her brush with death. A horrible feeling came over her. Even if Doe Sia knew the way, Emma wasn't sure she could walk even one mile to find her mother.

She began to think out loud, "Oh, I feel so weak. Can I make it? Can I keep up with Doe Sia? I will have to. Somehow I will do it. I must make it. Doe Sia will find the way, and I will never give up."

Emma was full of doubt. Everything she saw made her feel weak and helpless. Did she have the strength to make it back to her family? She would have to reach down inside of herself to find a way to do what looked like the impossible.

8

Snowy Prison

Emma crawled back into the tiny snowcave. The two girls lay next to each other and chewed on pieces of hide. They held snow in their mouths and let it melt. It gave them badly needed water. Hopefully a long night of rest would give them the much-needed strength to help them walk through the deep snow the next day.

Emma was deep in thought as she lay next to her new friend. She was sure the Heavenly Father had sent Doe Sia to save her life. She was sure all this was no accident and not just a coincidence. Doe Sia never would have seen Emma if the storm had not let up at just the right time. The Indian girl had to be in exactly the right place at exactly the right time to see Emma lying next to the fallen tree. Without perfect timing, Emma would have died in a matter of hours. Emma knew a miracle had happened for her.

Emma broke the silence. "Doe Sia, thank you for helping me. Thank you for saving my life. Without you I would be dead. I will do my best to keep up with you tomorrow."

"Emma, you can do it. We will walk the easiest way. Otterdog will help us. He runs right through deep snow. Snow will not stop us if we travel as the animals do. Now we must rest. We must be ready when morning comes," Doe Sia said soothingly.

After hearing Doe Sia's words, Emma felt better. Once again she lay quietly next to her friend and deep in thought. Otterdog snuggled under the buffalo robe and against Emma's feet. The snowcave blocked out all sounds. All that could be heard was the breathing of two girls and a dog. Emma silently said her prayers. She gave thanks for her life. She gave thanks for Doe Sia and Otterdog. She prayed for her mother and Peter. She prayed for all the suffering Saints trapped in the storm without food and without enough clothes and blankets.

After her prayer, Emma began to think about the Indian girl lying next to her. She remembered how afraid she was of Indians. She remembered praying that the pioneers would never see any Indians, ever. She remembered how she thought that all Indians were wild and dangerous. She had even had terrible dreams about Indian attacks. Now here she was lying next to Doe Sia, an Indian. Instead of being someone to be feared, Doe Sia was there to save Emma's life and to try to help her find her family. It was all so amazing to this Danish girl who had traveled thousands of miles and now was huddled in a snowcave in a vast wilderness.

While the girls slept that night, the snow started to fall once again. The wind began to blow. There was even some lightning and thunder. The girls heard nothing. The walls of the snowcave insulated them from all sounds. The girls woke up several times. Each time they changed positions, they laid close together to stay snug and warm. Their shared body heat was a lifesaver. Even Otterdog was doing his part to help the girls stay warm.

When Doe Sia began crawling from underneath the buffalo robe, Emma woke up. She felt stiff, but she had gained some much-needed strength. She pulled herself to her knees and crawled out of the snowcave and stood next to Doe Sia. Emma was shocked at the sight before her. Snow was falling again. There was some wind but not as much as during the main storm. Emma didn't know what to think. Would this force them to stay in the snowcave even longer? Would they have to continue to eat hide to stay alive? How long could they survive these horrible conditions? Emma hung her head in disbelief.

Doe Sia spoke softly, "The snow has returned, but we must leave. I saw the hills around us before we slept. I know I can find the river. The river will show us the way to your people. We can find the river. We will travel as the animals do."

Immediately Emma perked up. *Leave, find the river, the river will show us the way*—these were exciting words of great hope. Emma tingled with excitement. Could Doe Sia really find the river, even in the storm? Could it be possible? Emma was ready to try anything. She was ready to follow Doe Sia anywhere. She would do whatever it took to get back to Mother and Peter.

As the two girls prepared to leave the snowcave, Emma prayed, "Heavenly Father, please help us. Walk with us. Please guide Doe Sia. Protect Mother and Peter. Please help us find them today. Thank you for sending Doe Sia to me. Amen."

Doe Sia had a plan. Many times in her young life she had traveled with her people in the wintertime. Doe Sia was taught to find the easiest way to move in the snow. She saw how the wind had blown the snow away from the base of the mountainside. This left a shallow passage free of deep snow. A three- to five-foot drift ran next to this natural pathway. It

Emma and Doe Sia leave their snowcave
and begin the trek to find their people.

would be like walking in a ditch and it would be easy going. Best of all, the girls would not be walking in circles. This gave them a chance to find their way back to their people. But time would prove they were not out of danger yet.

Doe Sia told Emma they would share the warm buffalo robe. One would wear the buffalo robe while the other wore Emma's wool coat. After a while they would exchange with each other. At each rest stop they would huddle together for warmth in the buffalo robe.

Otterdog could hardly wait to get going. He was wild with excitement as the girls stood up to leave. When the girls started walking, Otterdog kept running ahead, turning, running back to the girls, and then running ahead again. His tail was wagging as fast as it would go. Emma walked just behind Doe Sia. Emma had the buffalo robe first. It was heavy. At the beginning she had trouble carrying it. She was still weak from her ordeal and from lack of food. As she walked, she chewed on a piece of hide. Every few minutes she grabbed a handful of snow, let it melt in her mouth, and swallowed the water it made.

When Doe Sia took her turn with the buffalo robe, Emma felt relieved. She could walk much easier without all that weight. Doe Sia stayed out in front, breaking trail and blocking the wind. Emma walked right behind her for protection from the biting cold. The girls traveled along the hillside for almost an hour. All was going well until they came to a steep wall of rock. The wall went straight up for twenty feet. Doe Sia decided this was a good place to rest. The girls sat down with their backs against the wall. They snuggled into the buffalo robe with only their faces showing. Otterdog lay next to Doe Sia and licked her hand and wagged his tail.

The rest felt so good to Emma. Before they stopped Emma was having trouble keeping up. She felt like begging her friend to stop. Lack of proper food was depriving Emma's body of its vital source of energy. Emma was beginning to wonder how much farther she could go. She closed her eyes and rested her head against the rock wall. No words were spoken as the girls rested. Emma almost fell asleep. As she began dozing off, Doe Sia started moving.

"We must go. Soon we will turn toward the river," Doe Sia said with confidence.

Emma gave Doe Sia the wool coat. She wrapped the buffalo robe around her shoulders and began walking behind her friend. Emma again felt dizzy and weak. Somehow she forced her legs into action. She automatically put one foot in front of the other. Her misery was turning into sheer agony.

The girls had walked only three minutes when they were startled by a sound like thunder. Emma looked up at exactly the right time. She was shocked to see what was coming over the rim of the rock wall high above them. Tons of snow were bearing down on the helpless travelers. Emma lunged forward and grabbed Doe Sia. She yanked her down next to the rock wall. Unbelievably they landed in a small depression in the wall. The avalanching snow poured down on the narrow pathway in front of them. It created a tremendous blast of wind.

The massive snowslide was over in seconds. Miraculously the girls were protected by the small depression in the rock. After the slide created the great blast of air, all fell silent. The girls were alive, entombed in a tiny natural snowcave. Doe Sia sat up and looked at their snowy prison. There was no door in this snowcave. Only a little dim light penetrated their small space.

"Doe Sia, are you all right? We're buried! We're going to die! What can we do?" Emma was screaming.

"I'm all right," Doe Sia screamed back. "Where is Otterdog?"

Doe Sia couldn't see Otterdog anywhere! She kept yelling her dog's name. She was afraid he was buried alive. As her eyes cleared and adjusted to the dim light, she desperately searched for Otterdog. Emma had fallen over when she yanked Doe Sia toward the wall. She slowly pulled herself to her hands and knees. She sat down and rubbed the snow from her eyes. When she put her left hand down, she felt something wonderful. Her heart thumped with joy.

"It's Otterdog! Doe Sia, he's here! Look, it's his tail!" Emma shouted as she held the dog's tail in her hand.

There it was. Otterdog's tail was sticking out of the wall of snow. He had not made it to the wall in time. He had been entombed by the roaring avalanche. Doe Sia quickly changed places with Emma. The Indian girl began clawing at the snow with her bare hands. The snow that had encased her dog was as hard as concrete. Quickly Doe Sia grabbed her knife from her hide pouch. With her knife she began cutting the hard snow away from Otterdog. She was careful not to injure him. First Doe Sia freed the dog's head so he could breathe. The pitiful animal looked like he was already dead. He didn't move.

Doe Sia quickly dug the snow from Otterdog's mouth and breathing passages. Then she continued working to free his body from its icy tomb. As she worked so frantically, her hands were creating pressure on the dog's sides. This caused Otterdog to cough and gag. His eyes opened. He had a look of utter terror in his eyes. Soon Doe Sia had Otterdog

in her arms. His tail wagged weakly and he licked
Doe Sia's face. Emma smiled and gently petted the
shaky dog. When she pulled her hand back, she saw
blood on her fingers. Otterdog had a deep cut on
his back.

Emma showed Doe Sia the blood on her hand.
The Indian girl quickly examined her dog. She hur-
riedly pulled a piece of hide from her bag and held
it against the dog's wound. Next she took a handful
of snow and placed it under the hide and against
the cut. She held Otterdog close to her body and
waited for the bleeding to stop.

The two girls sat back, catching their breath.
They had survived a monstrous killer. Everything
had happened with little warning. Without the protection of the depression in the rock wall, the girls
and Otterdog would have had no chance to survive.
They would have been crushed to death by tons of
rock-hard snow.

Doe Sia spoke slowly. "Thank you, Emma. You
saved me and Otterdog. The Great Spirit is here with
us. He is helping us live."

Emma thought about Doe Sia's words. Live? How could they live? They were buried alive under tons of snow. There was no door. Otterdog was hurt. Emma was horrified by this snowy prison. She thought she would lose control and panic any minute. How could Doe Sia be so sure they would get out of this horrible place alive?

"Emma," said Doe Sia, "we will escape this snow. We must be careful. We will find a way out. I know we can."

Even before their attempt to escape the snowy cavern, another miracle was about to happen for these young girls and Otterdog. A spectacular discovery was about to take place that would prove to be an answer to Emma's prayers. What was about to happen would truly be a gift from the Great Spirit.

9

Tunnel to Freedom

As Doe Sia looked for the safest and easiest way to dig out of their icy shelter, a chunk of snow fell from the wall of snow in front of the girls. It landed at their feet. Both girls were startled by the falling snow. Was the whole snowcave about to cave in on them? Would their lives be snuffed out? The two girls feared the worst! They had no idea what caused the chunk of snow to fall. Emma could hardly keep from screaming!

147

What appeared next in the wall right in front of them was a shock. The girls couldn't believe their eyes. Sticking out from the snow was the leg of an animal. When the leg began to flail at the snow, Emma screamed and pulled back as far as she could. She was about to panic and dive to one side.

Doe Sia quickly put her arm across Emma's waist and held her back. She motioned for Emma to sit still and be absolutely quiet. Emma calmed down a little but still sat curled up in shock. The animal's leg continued to thrash violently. In a matter of seconds another leg broke free from the snow. Now both legs were kicking wildly. Doe Sia kept her arm across Emma's body. Then she spoke.

"Emma, it's a buffalo! It's trapped and cannot escape. Stay still! Soon it will die! Don't move. Don't move."

Emma trembled, but Doe Sia's words kept her from panicking. The animal struggled violently for five minutes. Finally the frantic thrashing slowed. The entombed creature was in its final moments of life. The girls were witnessing death by suffocation.

At the end the two legs just quivered. The buffalo was dead. The legs fell limp and still. It was over. Doe Sia pulled her arm away from Emma. The two girls took a deep breath. They were gasping from all the excitement and shock of the last few minutes.

"Where did the buffalo come from? How did it get in the snow?" Emma stammered.

"The animal was caught by the sliding snow," Doe Sia explained. "Maybe he started the avalanche. My people have seen animals killed by snowslides. We have seen animals fall through the ice on lakes and streams and drown. This buffalo made a mistake. Now it is ours! The Great Spirit has sent this gift to us!"

Doe Sia let Emma hold Otterdog while she went to work. Doe Sia took her knife and began to cut the snow away from the animal's legs. Otterdog pulled away from Emma and cautiously sniffed at the protruding legs. He wasn't sure the animal was really dead.

"Stay back!" Doe Sia hollered as she pushed Otterdog away.

Emma pulled Otterdog back and slowly began petting the nervous dog as she watched Doe Sia work.

"Emma, it's a huge buffalo calf. There will be lots of fresh meat for us. Buffalo calves are good eating! We will not be hungry anymore!" Doe Sia laughed.

When Doe Sia had the rear half of the animal uncovered, she sat back to rest. She was out of breath from her frantic work. Emma motioned to Doe Sia to let her have the knife.

"Let me dig while you rest. I can help." Emma said.

Doe Sia watched her blonde friend go to work. She knew this was a good sign. Her friend had calmed down enough to offer her help. Emma could not believe how large the calf was. She had seen buffalo only from a distance before this happened. This was almost like living in a dream. Here she was lost in the wilderness, practically buried alive, and now she was digging a dead buffalo out of its snowy tomb.

Emma dug the best she could, but could not dig as well or as fast as Doe Sia could. When the Indian girl was rested, she took over from Emma. The girls kept taking turns digging and resting. When the snow was completely cleared from the dead animal, both girls rested for a few minutes. Then without warning, their rest was interrupted by a strange sound. It was a deep thumping sound. The gigantic pile of snow was settling and could cave in on the girls any second.

Quickly Doe Sia rolled to her hands and knees and desperately began digging into the snow next to her near the wall. She planned to dig along the wall until she found the edge of the avalanche. She hoped to be able to break through to the outside and safety.

"Emma, we have to get out of here!" Doe Sia shouted. "The snow is moving! It could cave in and bury us!"

The eerie sound of the snow moving stunned the girls. They forgot about the dead animal. They forgot about everything. Nothing would do them any good if they were completely buried. It would have been easy to panic, but that could mean certain death. While Doe Sia feverishly dug at the hard wall of snow, Emma huddled next to the rock with the buffalo robe clutched around her neck. Her eyes searched the snow in front of her. She stared at the dead buffalo calf. Had they wasted precious time uncovering the dead animal? Now would they be too late to save themselves? The more Emma thought these awful thoughts, the more terrified she became.

Emma's thoughts were interrupted by an even louder whumping sound. She let go of Otterdog and closed her eyes, pulling herself even closer to the rock wall. She turned her head away from Doe Sia. She began to tremble with fear. She was sure she was going to die any second.

When Emma opened her eyes again, she noticed Otterdog right next to her. The dog was digging into the snow at the exact spot where he had been buried. Emma remembered how his tail protruded from the snow. Now Emma was afraid that Otterdog was causing the snow to weaken and groan. Quickly she threw the buffalo robe off and reached

Emma watches Otterdog dig through the wall of snow.

to pull Otterdog back. As she reached down to grab the dog, she was startled by a strange sight. Were her eyes playing tricks on her again? She blinked several times and leaned over for a closer look.

My eyes are not fooling me! Emma thought. "Doe Sia, Doe Sia! Stop digging! Look, there's light right here. Otterdog is almost out! He found the way!" Emma was shrieking with joy.

Doe Sia immediately scrambled over Emma to take a look. She reached Otterdog at the exact second the dog was breaking through to the outside. On his belly the dog squirmed the last few inches through his tunnel to freedom. Outside, Otterdog started barking wildly. Doe Sia instantly began jabbing at the snow. She quickly enlarged the tunnel her dog had dug. In a short time the Indian girl was halfway into the opening. Suddenly Doe Sia's legs were gone. She was free too! She hollered for Emma to crawl through the new tunnel, but Emma hesitated. The tunnel looked so narrow. Fear gripped the young girl. She was terrified. Would the tunnel collapse and trap her in the narrow passage? Utter panic filled her mind. She was experiencing a severe attack of claustrophobia.

Doe Sia screamed at Emma to start crawling. Still Emma balked. Immediately Doe Sia squirmed back into the snowy cavern. She looked at Emma's troubled face and saw the terror in the girl's eyes.

"Emma, you must crawl out! You will die in here! Your only chance is to crawl out. Do you want to see your mother, or do you want to die here?"

"I want my mother," Emma murmured. "I want my mother."

"Then GO!" Doe Sia demanded.

Slowly Emma slid onto her stomach. She put her head into the tunnel and paused.

"GO!" screamed Doe Sia.

Emma began to wriggle into the snowy tunnel. Partway through the tunnel, she stopped. Doe Sia did not wait a second. She dove in behind Emma, put her hands on Emma's backside, and began pushing on Emma with all her might.

"Go, Emma, GO!" Doe Sia shouted.

Emma moved a little more. Doe Sia kept pushing. Suddenly Emma felt Otterdog licking her face. She opened her eyes. Her head was in the open. Frantically Emma propelled herself forward. A few seconds later she squirmed free. She raised herself to her hands and knees, breathless and trembling violently. Otterdog was racing around the girl barking loudly.

Seconds later Doe Sia emerged from the tunnel. Instantly she wheeled around and crawled back into the snowy space and pulled the buffalo robe out. She quickly wrapped the robe around her shaking friend.

"Emma, we're free! Otterdog saved us. He found the way!"

Emma sat with tears of joy running down her cheeks. She reached out and pulled Otterdog into her arms. She hugged the excited dog. Otterdog licked the tears from Emma's face. The girl held the heroic dog tightly. She put the hide bandage back in place. The bleeding was already stopping. The snowfall had stopped also. There were even patches of blue in the sky. Doe Sia was quickly working to make the tunnel larger. She was hacking away with her knife and pulling chunks of snow from the tunnel.

"We must get the buffalo! It is meat! It is food! It is another hide." Doe Sia proclaimed between her gasps for air.

In twenty minutes Doe Sia had more than tripled the size of the passage. She motioned for Emma to follow her into the cavern. This time Emma did not hesitate. On hands and knees the two girls each grabbed one of the buffalo's hind legs and began pulling. Inch-by-inch the girls moved the animal through the tunnel. They had to stop often to catch their breath and rest. The snow was helping the carcass to slide without getting stuck on rocks or roots. Still, moving the seven-hundred-pound animal was almost more than they could manage.

When the carcass was finally out in the open, the two exhausted friends sat leaning against the huge body. It felt good. The body was still warm. They were relieved to be finished with their labor.

Soon Doe Sia caught her breath and got on her knees next to the buffalo calf. She went right to work with her knife, making a cut into the animal's hide. Many times she had helped her mother process animal kills. First Doe Sia cut along the belly of the animal and cleaned out the body cavity. She quickly sliced strips of warm meat and began eating.

"Here, Emma, eat this! It will give you much strength. It is better than hide. The strength the fresh meat gives you will help you walk back to your mother."

Emma looked at the raw meat in her hand. It felt slimy. She had never eaten any raw meat before. She was so hungry and so desperate to find her mother that she would do anything Doe Sia told her to do. She was surprised at her first bite of the warm meat. It was tender and tasted so good. Emma ate three more strips.

"We must not eat too much now," Doe Sia warned. She continued her messy work. "Too much meat will cause pain and sickness. The storm is leaving.

We have meat. We have another hide. Now we must hurry before another storm comes."

Emma watched Otterdog gobble up the meat he was given. He excitedly sniffed the huge carcass. Emma was amazed by Doe Sia's skill. The Indian girl was working as fast as she could. She had the hide free of the body and was cutting the most tender meat into strips. She filled her hide bag full of delicious meat. She scraped the hide as clean as she could. She had cut the huge hide down to the size that would fit Emma snugly as a robe.

When the hasty work was done, Doe Sia handed Emma her new robe. Emma gave Doe Sia's robe back to her. Both girls wrapped themselves in their hides and sat back for a short rest. They each enjoyed a strip of raw tenderloin. Doe Sia examined Otterdog's wound and packed more snow under the piece of hide even though the bleeding had stopped.

"Doe Sia, you can do anything. You did that work so fast. This meat is delicious. I'm feeling stronger already. You are a great friend. Now I know we can make it and all because of you. I'm glad Otterdog is getting better. He is the greatest dog in the world."

"Emma, you're my friend too. You pulled me back from the snowslide. You saved Otterdog. We will make it together."

During their short rest Emma stared up at the bright blue sky. She saw layers of storm clouds drifting east. Soon the whole sky would be clear. The sun would shine down on the entire landscape. Emma said a silent prayer of thanksgiving. She had so much to be thankful for: Doe Sia's help, surviving the avalanche, fresh meat to eat, a new buffalo robe, and a clear blue sky. The young Danish girl had a warm feeling from head to toe. Now she was sure they would find her family soon.

Doe Sia realized time was important. She knew they would have to move as fast as possible over difficult terrain. She knew that mountain weather could change in a matter of minutes. There was no way of knowing what might be coming from west of this mountain valley. Better than Emma, Doe Sia knew that their ordeal was far from over. The Indian girl knew all the hazards that threatened the two of them and her dog. Now they had to make good decisions or they could face death again. They could not afford a single mistake.

10

Lifesaving Banks

As Doe Sia stood up to prepare to leave, she suddenly pulled back toward Emma. A loud groaning sound filled the air and the whole avalanche area next to them caved in on the girls' snowy prison. They had escaped just in time. They never would have survived this final collapse of the tons of snow.

"Doe Sia, we would have been killed! Let's get out of here before another avalanche comes!" Emma begged.

Without a word Doe Sia led Emma away from the dangerous hillside. She knew too that there would be no surviving the powerful force packed by such a monster. Going was slow. The snow was deep. Doe Sia carefully circled around the deepest snowdrifts. The welcomed sunshine felt so good. The girls trudged through the snow in silence. Otterdog bounded ahead crashing through the drifts until he became exhausted. Then he fell back and walked in the tracks made by the girls.

Doe Sia and Emma took turns breaking trail through the deep snow. They were breathing hard as they battled through the huge drifts. Doe Sia had just taken the lead when she unexpectedly took a turn and angled for a nearby hill. The slope ahead was nearly bare. The wind had blown it clear of most of the snow. Doe Sia's plan was to walk in switchback fashion up the hillside and in that way decrease the steepness of the climb. At the top she hoped to be able to see landmarks that would guide them to the river.

The weary girls paused at the base of the hill for only a few minutes and then began their trek upward. The climb up the hillside was slow. The girls had to stop often to catch their breath. Otter-dog went scampering right to the top with ease only to come racing back down to the girls. He circled the girls, barking loudly and then bounded right back up the hill. Emma wished it was that easy for her.

The higher the girls climbed, the farther they could see. The sun on the white blanket of snow was nearly blinding. The girls squinted, and their eyes watered. It was almost impossible to see anything looking west where the sun was right in their eyes. One hundred feet from the top, Doe Sia stopped. She sat down on the buffalo robe and motioned for Emma to sit next to her. She pulled out some strips of meat and handed Emma some. Doe Sia sat back with her eyes closed and chewed a strip of meat.

"We will be at the top soon. I think we will learn a lot when we look down from this hill. I think I know this hill. I think I know this place," Doe Sia explained calmly.

"Oh, Doe Sia, do you mean it? You know this very hill? You know where we are?" Emma bubbled on happily. "How soon will we reach the river? How long will it take?"

"Maybe we will see the river today. The sun is low in the sky. Soon darkness will visit the land. We will make a shelter. We will sleep. When Grandfather Sun returns again, we will follow the river to your people."

Emma marveled at Doe Sia's words. The Indian girl spoke so confidently and so calmly. Emma wondered how Doe Sia could be so calm. Why wasn't she more excited? Emma could hardly sit still, but Doe Sia understood they needed to be careful and not move too fast. One hasty mistake could result in injury or death. The Indian girl knew that every move had to be made with caution and care.

Emma's thoughts turned to her family. *How far away are they? Are Mother and Peter still alive? Do they think I'm dead?* The young girl offered a silent prayer. *Dear Heavenly Father, let Mother and Peter*

live. I love them so much. Please help me find them,
please. Thank you. Amen.

Emma didn't know it, but the rescuers from Salt
Lake City had arrived in time to save many lives.
The wagon loads of food, warm clothes, and blankets had come just in time for most. For others, it
was too late. With the ground frozen solid, it was
impossible to bury the dead. There were many devastating heartaches. Almost every family had lost
at least one loved one. Some had lost more.

Peter and Emma's mother had lived through the
ordeal. They had done better than most people in
Captain Willie's company. When Elder Kimball did
not return with Emma, Peter came up with his own
plan: If the Martin company was still strung out
behind, why couldn't he go back himself and look
for Emma? If they couldn't find Emma, at least they
could help those who needed them. What good did
it do to stay here and just hope for the best. It was
time to do something.

When he told his mother about his idea, she
agreed. "Yes, Peter, we'll both go back. Now we have

food and clothes. We can look for Emma, and we can help those who need us. Peter, I have been praying for Emma every minute. I know Elder Kimball hasn't found her. Maybe he's still searching. We don't know. Let's go, Peter."

"Mother, I have been praying too. I think Emma is alive. I will search all the way to the end of the line if I have to. We will find her, I promise."

Even as Peter spoke, he had a feeling of great guilt. *Why hadn't he tried to find Emma before this? Why didn't he think about dropping back as soon as Emma was lost? Why did he leave it up to Elder Kimball? Why didn't he go back with him to look for his little sister?* Peter felt terrible. He was blaming himself for Emma's loss. He would never be able to forgive himself if she was dead.

Doe Sia and Emma had hiked the short distance to the top of the hill. They looked to the southwest where Doe Sia thought they would see the river. It was very hard to see with all the glare of the sunlight on the snow. Emma squinted and shaded her eyes but could not see a river anywhere.

"Doe Sia, where is the river? I don't see a river!" Emma was frightened.

"Emma, this is not the hill. I am wrong, but I know where we are. The river is beyond that far ridge. The road is there too."

"How long will it take us to go over that ridge? If it takes too long, I'll never find my family! They will be gone!" Emma started sobbing.

"We will rest tonight. We will leave at daylight tomorrow. Tomorrow we will find the river before darkness comes. We can travel faster than your family. Emma, we will find them."

Emma didn't say a word. She felt horrible. She thought they would never make it now. All her hopes were shattered. She wondered if she could believe anything Doe Sia said. Emma was dejected and felt like giving up.

"Emma, darkness comes soon. When Grandfather Sun leaves, it will be very cold. We need shelter. We must go down now!"

The Indian girl could tell that Emma was sad and disappointed. She knew the girl wanted to see the river and find her family today. She also knew they needed shelter and a good rest. She started immediately for the trees below them.

At the bottom Doe Sia said nothing but went right to work. There were no drifts large enough to make a snowcave. The Indian girl found three bare branches hanging from a spruce tree. She snapped them off and quickly used a piece of hide to tie their ends together. She set them up like a tripod. Next she began breaking spruce branches from the small trees around her. She started weaving them into the tripod. She ordered Emma to break off more branches.

At first Emma worked like a robot. She seemed to be just going through the motions. However, as the shelter started taking shape, Emma became more interested. She was witnessing another amazing skill that Doe Sia had. Emma even began to forget her utter disappointment at not finding the river.

The Indian girl's hands wove the branches tightly together, forming a barrier against any wind or snow. When she was finished, she motioned for

Emma to help break off more branches. These branches Doe Sia used to make a covering over the snowy floor inside the wickiup shelter. This shelter would be very cozy and comfortable. They would each have their own hide bed and be insulated from the cold snow on the ground by their spruce-branch mattress.

The girls followed Otterdog into the newly made shelter. The sun was already down. The temperature was dropping rapidly. Each girl rolled up in her own hide bed. Emma threw her wool coat over her new hide. The girls agreed to sleep together if they couldn't stay warm in their own beds. The two friends ate buffalo meat and melted snow in their mouths for water. Doe Sia gave Otterdog his share of the delicious meat and made sure his wound was healing well. The two girls talked quietly about all that had happened to them. Doe Sia kept telling Emma that she would see her mother soon. She told Emma that she was doing well and that she should not give up now.

When the girls became quiet, Emma silently said her prayers. After her prayers she began to think about the next day. *The valley is very wide. The snow is knee deep. The ridge on the other side is steep. Will I ever make it all the way to the ridge and then climb to the top? Will I be able to keep up and keep going? I will do everything I can to keep going until I find Mother and Peter.*

When Emma finally fell asleep, she dreamed and dreamed. In one dream she was following Doe Sia up the ridge. Just when they reached the top, they saw another ridge even higher than the first one. This went on and on until Emma finally woke up. She felt herself shaking. She had almost forgotten where she was and who she was with. Then it all came back to her. The long, long night seemed to never end.

When morning finally arrived, the groggy girls were up, preparing to leave. While they pulled their buffalo robes out of the shelter, they chewed on buffalo meat. It was well below freezing in this high mountain valley. Their buffalo robes felt good. In a matter of minutes the girls were on their way. Otter-dog's wound looked much better. He bounded through the snow out in front of the two girls. Progress was slow, but it felt good to be moving again.

Very few words were spoken. The girls plodded on in silence. The weather was still clear. The snow came up to their knees. Again the girls took turns breaking a trail. Ahead a row of trees marked the bank of a small stream. One huge dead tree stood tall above the rest. Its branches were like bare arms reaching into the blue sky. Doe Sia had used this dead tree to guide her to the creek and to keep her on course to the best route up the ridge ahead.

As the girls neared the massive dead tree, Doe Sia spoke. "We have gone far. Soon we will climb the ridge. We must rest here. We must eat. We will drink water from the creek."

Doe Sia walked straight to the creek. On the way down to the water she stomped a path in the deep snow. She let Emma drink first. Emma drank and drank. The water was wonderful. As she took her

Doe Sia shoves Emma into the creek
to avoid being hit by a massive tree.

last sip, a loud crack shattered the peaceful scene. Instantly Emma felt herself being shoved into the stream face first. Doe Sia landed in the water next to Emma. Then an even louder sound rattled Emma's eardrums. The enormous tree had slammed into the ground inches above the girls' heads. Only the creek banks had saved them from being crushed to death. Doe Sia's quick thinking and instant action had saved both girls from certain death. It all happened in an instant. Slowly the shaken girls crawled from the creek. Now they were wet and cold. They shivered and shook. When they looked around, they realized how close they had come to being crushed to death.

"Hurry!" Doe Sia yelled. "Wipe away the water! Wipe it from your body and dress! We must get warm and dry."

Emma acted quickly. She wiped the water away. She wrapped the buffalo robe around her body and sat down on the fallen tree. Emma went into utter shock. She was unable to think clearly. Her vision became blurry. Her eyes could not focus on anything. She sat staring straight ahead. Doe Sia sat next to her dazed friend. Emma said nothing.

Doe Sia broke the silence, "The Great Spirit is still here with us. Again he saved us from death. We are still alive. We must drink water and eat meat. We must climb the ridge. I know the river is close. Emma, eat! Drink more water! Forget the tree!"

It seemed like Emma had heard nothing Doe Sia had said. She just sat staring at the creek. It seemed as though the shocked girl was in a trance.

"Emma, eat! Drink! We must leave! We must go to the river. We will find your mother."

Emma stood up and moved stiffly to the creek. She kneeled and drank. She climbed the bank and sat back down on the fallen tree. The Indian girl handed her some meat. Emma stared at it and began chewing on a piece. Still she sat staring straight ahead. Doe Sia realized once again that there was something wrong with Emma.

"We have to go now!" Doe Sia hollered. "Your mother is nearby. You will see your mother soon."

The Indian girl knew Emma was shocked by the near disaster. She knew that they had to leave this place immediately. She hoped walking would make Emma feel better. Doe Sia started trudging toward the ridge. Slowly Emma stood and began to follow her friend. The word *mother* caused Emma to obey Doe Sia's commands and start moving again.

As the girls waded through the deep snow, Emma began to come out of her shock. She was warming up and drying out. The food and water had helped a lot. She was even beginning to look at the slope ahead. *Will I be able to make it to the top? Will my mother be on the other side? What if the handcarts are gone? What if I am already too late?* Emma's mind was flooded with thoughts and questions. She was interrupted by Doe Sia.

"We will be at the top of the ridge when Grandfather Sun is high above our heads. Then we will see the river. Emma, I know this place," Doe Sia said confidently.

The way Doe Sia spoke made Emma think that the Indian girl really did know where they were.

Then Emma remembered the hill that Doe Sia thought she knew and was wrong. Would she be wrong again? Emma hoped and prayed that this time Doe Sia would be right. She realized that following Doe Sia was her only chance. She knew that she would have to follow her friend wherever she went. Soon Emma would know for herself what lay on the other side of the ridge. Soon she would know if there was any hope of ever finding Mother and Peter. This had to be it.

11

The Answer

The girls took a final rest at the base of the ridge. They sat close together wrapped tightly in their buffalo robes. There was no wind. The warm sunshine felt so good. Emma rested her head against a tree and closed her eyes to say a silent prayer.

Please, Heavenly Father, help me climb this ridge. I'm so tired. Please let this be the right way. Please let me find Mother and Peter. Please let them be alive and safe. I love them so much. Thank you, Heavenly Father.

Doe Sia spoke softly. "We must eat and drink. The climb will be long, and we will need strength. The buffalo meat has saved us and now it will give us strength to climb. The buffalo calf came from the Great Spirit. The Great Spirit is with us guiding our feet."

"Doe Sia, you are so good to me. You saved me from freezing to death. Now you are helping me find my family. Thank you, Doe Sia, thank you. I will climb to the ridge. I will make it to the top. I can do it," Emma said as she embraced her new "sister."

Doe Sia smiled at Emma. The girls sat back quietly, each of them in deep thought. Above them the ridge rose into the clear blue sky. The temperature was below freezing, but the sun made it feel much warmer than it really was. Their rest ended when Doe Sia stood up and motioned for Emma to follow her. Otterdog was already on the way.

The first part of the climb seemed very easy. Doe Sia cut gradual angles up the slope. At the end of each angle she switched back the other way. Doe Sia knew this would make it easier for Emma to keep going all the way to the top. This was the same way the girls had climbed the hill the day before. The snow on this climb was only ankle deep. The girls had to be sure of each foothold. It would be easy to slip and start sliding.

Halfway up the ridge Emma began to tire. She was slipping more and more as time passed. She began to worry. How much farther was it to the top? She kept telling herself she could make it. She did her best to keep up with Doe Sia but was falling behind more and more with each step. Doe Sia noticed Emma slipping often and dropping behind. The Indian girl slowed her pace. Just when Emma thought she couldn't take another step, Doe Sia stopped and sat down.

"We are more than halfway. We have done better than I thought we could. Let's eat and drink. We can rest. Soon we will be at the top," Doe Sia stated confidently.

For Emma, it felt so good to stop. She slumped to the ground with her buffalo robe protecting her from the snow. She took a deep breath and relaxed.

The buffalo meat tasted better than ever, but best of all she could rest. She shared a piece of meat with the faithful Otterdog. Emma loved this good animal.

Doe Sia said, "Emma, when we get to the top, we will see the river. The road will be there too. I know this ridge. My people are back the other way. I know this land. Maybe we will see your people on the road. If we don't, we will follow the ridge top until we find them. Then we will go down. The ridge will be bare and easy to walk."

Emma wanted so much to believe Doe Sia's words. She was afraid to ask how far the river might be from the ridge. She knew her energy was running out. She already felt very weary. By the time she reached the top, she knew she would be completely exhausted.

The short rest helped, but Emma hurt all over when she pulled herself to her feet. Doe Sia motioned Emma to go first. She knew Emma would do better in the lead. She told Emma to go slowly and stop to rest whenever she needed it. For Emma, right away it felt better to be out in front. Emma concentrated on just putting one foot in front of the other. She was thankful that the snow was only a few inches deep. Slow but steady progress was made.

Near the top of the ridge, Doe Sia came up alongside Emma. The two girls reached the crest of the ridge together and were instantly hit by a cold, damp wind. When they looked into the valley, they were shocked to see a dense layer of fog that filled the entire valley. It was impossible to see any of the valley floor. Emma let out a weak groan of disappointment.

"Emma, there is fog, but it is moving. Grandfather Sun will chase the fog from the valley. Soon we will see the river and the road. We have climbed well. We will use this time to rest. We will be ready when Grandfather Sun sends the fog away," Doe Sia said soothingly.

Otterdog seemed to know Emma was sad. The dog licked Emma's hand. He even made her smile. Doe Sia led Emma back the way they had just come and below the ridge crest out of the wind. The girls hunkered down in their buffalo robes to wait for the fog to leave. It felt so good to rest. After a snack, Emma even dozed off for a few minutes. The Indian girl knew her friend was weary and needed this rest badly. Now she wondered if Emma could ever make it all the way to the river and the road below the ridge. Doe Sia knew she would have to find a way to help her friend make the final distance.

Doe Sia's thoughts turned to her own mother and her own people. She longed to return to her people. She knew her mother would be worried about her. She also knew her mother would want her to help Emma and would be as proud of her as she was the day Doe Sia saved Little Squirrel.

It happened so fast. Suddenly the fog bank began rolling out of the valley and over the ridge. The air became damper than ever as the fog blew by the girls.

"Emma, the fog is leaving! Soon we will see the river and the road! Finish your meat. We must be ready to leave," the excited Doe Sia said.

Emma was stiff and sore as she huddled close to the side of the ridge. She quickly chewed the last bit of meat and gave Otterdog a piece. A strange fear came over her as she watched the fog blow by. She dreaded the moment when she would be able to see into the valley. Would she be disappointed again? What if there was no river and no road? Would there be another ridge to climb? These troubling thoughts made Emma want Doe Sia to look first.

Emma silently said a final prayer, *Dear Heavenly Father, please let us see the road. Please let me find my mother and brother. I love them so much. Please let them be there.*

Doe Sia stood on the ridge watching the fog thin out. It was as if a giant curtain was being lifted from the valley floor. Gradually the Indian girl could see the valley come into view.

"The river! There it is! It's the river!" Doe Sia shrieked. "The road must be close by."

Emma couldn't believe her ears. The river? The road? Could it be true? A surge of adrenaline roared through the girl's body. She rose to her feet with

ease and rushed to Doe Sia's side. There it was! The
Sweetwater River was like an enormous snake wind-
ing through the blanket of snow. Frantically Emma
searched for any sign of life, but the valley seemed
to be completely deserted. There was no one in
sight. Were the handcarts gone? Had they stopped
before reaching this valley? Which way were they?
Where were they? These questions and more were
racing through Emma's mind.

A chill of disappointment shot through the
dejected girl. Where could Mother be? She was so
happy to see the river, but what good did it do?
Which way should they go? More troubling thoughts
tumbled out of Emma.

Emma looked at Doe Sia. She wondered why the
Indian girl didn't say anything. Doe Sia was just
standing there staring intently at the valley floor.
Her eyes seemed to be searching every inch of the
area near the river. Doe Sia stood in one place for a
long time without moving an inch or making a
sound. Emma realized her friend did not want to be

distracted, but what was she looking at? Could she see something Emma could not see?

At last Doe Sia motioned for Emma to follow her. The girl and her dog walked west along the ridge top. The ridge was completely bare of snow. The walking was easy. Emma wondered if Doe Sia had seen something. How did she know they should walk west and not east? Did something tell Doe Sia this was the right way? The Indian girl said nothing. Yes, Doe Sia had seen something, but she wasn't sure what it was. She remained silent. She did not want Emma to get her hopes up and then be disappointed again.

The girls walked almost half a mile before Doe Sia came to a stop. Once more the girl carefully scanned the area near the river. There it was! The strange shape in the snow was easier to see from here!

Doe Sia finally spoke. "Look, down there near the river. Look at the snow near the small trees."

Emma looked where Doe Sia told her to look. At first she didn't see anything unusual. Then her eyes caught sight of something that sent a chill down her spine. She stared harder and harder, thinking it must be a mistake. It wasn't a mistake! Her eyes were not playing tricks on her! There in the snow the wheel of a handcart was barely visible. The handcart was laying on its side, abandoned.

"Doe Sia, it's a handcart. It's a handcart! You found it! You found it! My people passed that place. They are farther west. Let's go. Let's go!"

"Wait," Doe Sia cautioned. "We will go, but we must be careful. If we go down too soon, the snow will be deep. We must stay on the ridge where the walking is easy. We must not go down until we see more signs of your people. In winter my people always travel where there is little snow, the same as the animals do. We will too."

Emma tingled all over with excitement. She even forgot how tired she was. As Doe Sia began walking, Emma followed her so closely she nearly stepped on her friend's heels. Many thoughts flooded Emma's mind. Was her mother just ahead? What would she see around the next bend in the river? Emma had an overwhelming feeling that she was close to a great discovery. She hoped and prayed that she was right.

Without warning, Doe Sia stopped. Emma turned sharply to avoid running into her friend. This time the Indian girl was looking off to the southeast. Otterdog was barking excitedly and his tail wagged wildly. Doe Sia pointed to a distant ridge. There a column of smoke drifted upward.

"Emma, my people are there! Soon we will find your family. Soon I can return to my mother! The Great Spirit has guided our feet! Soon we will both be safe! Now we must travel quickly."

Doe Sia's words thrilled Emma. Both of them would find their families and be safe! Emma's prayers were being answered. She felt like running and jumping. Suddenly she realized that she still couldn't be sure her mother was near or even still alive. This sobering thought took the edge off her great joy.

Doe Sia immediately headed for a large mass of rock that stuck straight up out of the ridge top. She knew she could circle around this barrier and then have a clear view of much more of the valley where the river made a sharp turn. Doe Sia had to carefully pick her way through loose rock to get around these tall jagged rocks. She took her time to make sure of each foothold and to avoid a slip. A fall here could cause a severe injury. Otterdog was leading the way.

Doe Sia finally made it safely around the rocky barrier. There she stood looking at a wonderful sight in the valley below. She could hardly keep still, but she didn't say a word. She didn't want Emma to get excited and lose her concentration and fall. Doe Sia and Otterdog stood absolutely still as Emma came up next to them. All Doe Sia did was point to the river valley stretched out at their feet. There it was! A large camp of handcarts was hugging the edge of the river. There were two large supply wagons parked in the center of the camp. People were moving about as they worked to set up tents and build fires.

Emma shouted, "My people! My people! We found my people! Thank you, Heavenly Father, thank you.

Emma and Doe Sia are able to see the camp at last.

Mother, here I am, I'm coming! Thank you, Doe Sia, you were right. Thank you! Thank you! Let's go! Let's find Mother and Peter."

Emma threw her arms around Doe Sia and gave her a hard hug.

Doe Sia cautioned, "Emma, we will go, but we must stay on the ridge until we are above the camp. Then you can go down. Then I can return to my people. We still must be careful. We are high above the valley. We are tired. I can see the safest and fastest way to the camp. Follow me."

Emma was delirious with excitement, but she obediently followed Doe Sia. As they walked, the ridge began to slope down toward the camp. Overwhelming joy and relief flooded over Emma as she bounced along. She tingled all over! She could hardly hold herself back! She wanted to run and shout and wave her arms! She didn't even know if this was the Willie company or the Martin company. She couldn't think clearly.

When the girls approached the spot directly above the camp, Doe Sia stopped. Two people were struggling to pull a hardcart the last little way into the camp. Doe Sia pointed toward the two who labored so hard to move the loaded handcart. Emma hadn't even noticed them. When she did look, she thought her eyes were fooling her.

The girl let out a shriek, "It's Peter! It's my brother!"

Even her loudest screams could not be heard by anyone below her. The sound was carried away by the wind blowing up the ridge. Doe Sia grabbed Emma by the arm and pointed to the snowy slope at their feet. It led straight to the slowly moving handcart. The Indian girl dropped her buffalo robe from her shoulders. She motioned for Emma to take her robe off too. Emma was hardly able to concentrate. She couldn't take her eyes off the scene below her. Quickly Doe Sia laid Emma's buffalo robe on the snow just inches below the crest of the ridge. Here the snow was crusted and covered with two inches of loose powdery snow. There were no obstacles on the route all the way to the valley floor.

Doe Sia spoke firmly. "Sit on the hide. Put your feet forward. Hold the hide back over your feet. You will slide slowly and safely to the valley. I have slid like this many times."

Emma turned and looked at Doe Sia. She knew the Indian girl was not coming with her on this last part of the trip. Tears flowed down Emma's cheeks. She knew it was time to say good-bye to the one who saved her life and brought her back to her family. Emma hugged Doe Sia and sobbed one thank-you after another. Then she dropped on her knees and gave Otterdog a final hug and handed him a piece of meat. Otterdog licked Emma's face one last time. Then Emma turned and sat down on the buffalo robe. Doe Sia pulled the front edge of the buffalo hide up to Emma's hands. It made the hide take on the shape of a crude toboggan.

"Emma, hang on! Lean back. You will slide safely down. You will not slide too fast," Doe Sia shouted final directions. "There is nothing in your way. Your brother will see you. Hang on!"

Emma followed directions perfectly. Doe Sia gave Emma a shove and away she slid. It was an amazing sight. Emma's blonde hair was blowing straight back. She glided smoothly on the crusted snow. As she passed the halfway point, she began yelling Peter's name. Seconds later Peter stopped. He looked around to find the source of the noise. He thought he heard someone calling his name. Then he spotted a strange sight. Something was sliding down the ridge. Loose snow was blowing back over Emma and hiding her from view. What was this strange thing coming toward Peter?

As Emma's makeshift toboggan slowed, the snow began to settle. Now Peter could see that a person was sitting on the sliding object. Then he heard Emma's voice loud and clear. Peter yelled out Emma's name. The boy sprinted wildly from the handcart. The deep snow couldn't slow his frantic pace. In no time Peter reached Emma and had his little sister in his arms and was whirling her around and around.

"Emma! Emma! You're alive! Praise the Heavenly Father. Emma, I love you! I love you. We thought you were . . ." Peter couldn't finish. He broke down in tears of unbelievable joy.

"Oh, Peter, I love you! I love you! But where is Mother? Is Mother all right?"

Before Peter had time to answer, someone came running from the camp. This woman had been watching for Peter's return. It was Emma's mother. She was running so fast that she slipped and fell. Before she could get up, Emma and Peter were running to meet her. The three of them met in a joyful reunion. They threw their arms around each other. The cries of joy could be heard all the way to the camp. They danced around and around. Many minutes passed before any of them could speak. Over and over they told each other of their love. They shouted thanks for answered prayers. This had to be the happiest day of their lives!

Before other people reached the joyful family, Emma's mother asked her daughter questions. "How did you stay alive so long? Where did you get the buffalo hide? How did you find your way back? Who helped you?"

In the excitement Emma had forgotten everything. Emma turned and looked up at the ridge. She pointed upward. There on the ridge top against the clear sky stood an Indian girl and her dog. Doe Sia had a singing heart. The Indian girl was full of happiness for her blonde-haired friend. Now she, too, could return to her mother and find her happiness.

"Mother, there she is. There's Doe Sia, the one who saved my life." Between sobs, Emma said, "She helped me find you. She risked her life to save mine."

Emma, Peter, and Mother looked up at the girl and her dog. With tears streaming down her face, Emma waved farewell to Doe Sia and Otterdog. Emma's ordeal was over. It had all ended so suddenly. Emma's love for Doe Sia was real. She would always remember and love this amazing Indian girl.

Doe Sia waved back to Emma. Then the Indian girl slowly wrapped her buffalo robe around her shoulders, turned, and disappeared down the other side of the ridge. Doe Sia and Otterdog were headed home. Their job was done.

Doe Sia waves good-bye after Emma
is reunited with her family.

Epilogue

When Emma, Peter, and Mother finally calmed
down, they walked into the camp to share their joy
with the company of pioneers. Emma was relieved
to find Katrina and her family safe in the camp. As
Emma warmed herself by a fire, she was given food
and water. She was asked to tell the whole story of
her survival in the fierce blizzard. Emma tried hard
to remember every detail. There were gaps in her
story when she suffered from hypothermia and
could not remember what Doe Sia had told her
when they lay in the first snowcave. Her story would

be told in full after the company reached Salt Lake City.

Doe Sia had to survive one more night before she could travel the final distance to her people. She, too, was asked to tell her story to her family and the elders of the tribe. Doe Sia's mother was once more proud of her daughter for saving the life of someone who needed her. Again Doe Sia and Otter-dog were the center of attention among their people. Both Doe Sia and Emma hoped to meet again one day. It is very possible that they did since the Bannock Indian people roamed all over the West before they were forced to live on a reservation at Fort Hall, Idaho.

Eventually all the surviving handcart people were rescued by wagons from Salt Lake City. Both the Willie company and the Martin company had endured unbelievable hardships in the state we now call Wyoming. The violent early winter storm had been very hard on these courageous and devoted Saints. Stories of bravery and sacrifice abounded. Many young men even paid with their lives.

The rescuers loaded the weak, the aged, and the injured on the wagons for the final part of the journey to Salt Lake City. Many of the handcart pioneers continued to pull their handcarts all the way to Salt Lake City without assistance. Peter, for one, pulled his family's cart all the way and at the same time continued to help those who were struggling to pull their carts. Young men like Peter would be praised and honored by the church leaders for their heroic dedication.

It was November 9 when the last of Captain Willie's handcart pioneers reached Salt Lake City. The Martin company would endure three more weeks of agony before they arrived on November 30.

Not enough can be said about the bravery, the faith, and the courage of these hundreds of Saints who undertook an agonizing journey to follow their dream of freedom to worship as they chose. There is much to learn from these hardy and faithful pioneers. Their example is worthy of our deepest respect regardless of our own religious convictions.

Long before the Saints encountered the hardships of travel in the state now called Wyoming, a reporter for the *Council Bluffs Eagle,* a newspaper in Nebraska Territory, wrote this column on August 26, 1856.

> It may seem to some that these people endure great hardships in traveling hundreds of miles on foot, drawing carts behind them. This is a mistake, for many informed me that after the first three days of travel, it requires little effort for two or three men or women to draw the light handcart with its moderate load of cooking utensils and baggage. The best evidence of their sincerity is in the fact that they are willing to endure the fatigues and privations of a journey so lengthy. This is enthusiasm. This is heroism indeed. Though we cannot coincide with them in their beliefs, it is impossible to restrain our admiration of their self-sacrificing devotion to the principles of their faith.

This reporter's sincere account of what he observed is very moving indeed. For us modern Americans it is always easy to look back and say, "If only they would have . . ." "They should have known . . ." "Why didn't they prepare for the worst?" Such criticism comes easily. Passing judgment is a temptation, but learning from this example of true faith and courage can prove to be a great inspiration for all of us.

Ken Thomasma, a seasoned teacher, principal, and media specialist, now spends his time as a writing workshop leader and professional storyteller. He is concerned that children have accurate information about Americans who lived in the West before white settlers came. A careful researcher as well as a storyteller, Ken checks out details and descriptions with tribal leaders so that his material is not only historically accurate but also welcomed and appreciated by Indians themselves.

There are now eight books in the popular **Amazing Indian Children** series. Three of the books have won the Wyoming Children's Book Award: *Naya Nuki, Pathki Nana,* and *Moho Wat.* The books have also been nominated for the Colorado Children's Book Award and the Colorado Blue Spruce Award. *Naya Nuki* was nominated for the Utah Children's Book Award. The books have been translated into

Japanese, Danish, Dutch, Norwegian, and Eskimo dialects for Greenland. Currently a movie is being made of the *Naya Nuki* story.

Ken, his wife, Bobbi, and the younger Thomas-mas—Dan, Cathy, grandson Oliver, and grand-daughter Melissa—enjoy spectacular views of ever-changing scenery from their homes located on the south border of Grand Teton National Park in Jackson Hole, Wyoming.

Agnes Vincen Talbot's love of the native American West began in her childhood days growing up in Boise, Idaho. After developing her significant natural talent, she moved to Connecticut, continued her art studies for fourteen years, and then returned to Boise. She is a disciplined art historian who insists on authenticity and demanding detail in her sculpture and paintings. Her intricate illustrations in this book reflect her love for the rich history of the American West. This is the second book she has illustrated. Her bronze of Sacajawea and her baby is featured on the U.S. Mint Web Page in connection with the new Sacajawea dollar coin to be issued in the year 2000.